The Connemara *Whirlwind*

First published in 1990 by
Poolbeg Press Ltd,
123 Baldoyle Industrial Estate,
Dublin 13,
Ireland
E-mail: poolbeg@poolbeg.com
www.poolbeg.com
Reissued 2001

© Ann Henning 1990

A catalogue record for this book is available from the British Library.

ISBN 1 85371 079 2

Cover Photography by Michael Edwards
Cover design by Vivid
Printed by The Guernsey Press Ltd,
Vale, Guernsey, Channel Islands.

The
Connemara
Whirlwind

Ann Henning

POOLBEG

To Cashel Grey, my first Connemara pony, and her numerous successors, who between them have provided the inspiration and experience necessary to write this book.

Contents

The Cuaifeach

1

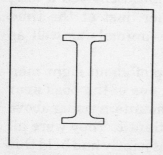t was one of those glorious early summer days in Connemara that make winter appear like nothing but a bad dream. The sun shone on glittering blue waters, the bogs had a soft green cover of fresh new grass, and even the bare mountainsides were enlivened by dashes of bright colour. The air was clear and gentle, resounding with bird-song and the humming of bees, and sweetly scented by a host of wild flowers.

Seeing it now, it was hard to imagine that only a few weeks before, this country had been hostile and grey, lashed by vicious Atlantic gales, washed by torrents of rain. People had run for shelter, huddled in front of turf fires. On the mountains animals had shivered, lean and shaggy, weakened by the lack of grass.

Then suddenly one day...winter was over. The miracle had occurred, this year as every year, and as usual in this part of the world, it happened overnight. Storms and chills were soon forgotten, as Connemara enjoyed a long spell of hot sunny weather, just at the time when all its inhabitants—animals as well as humans—needed it most.

This afternoon, a group of about eight men were working the turf on one of the bogs near the foot of Cashel Hill, a mountain rising above a sheltered inlet of the Atlantic. They were all Cashel men whose families jointly had held this plot for generations.

In Connemara, as in other parts of rural Ireland, each man cuts his own turf to keep his family warm in winter. It is a seasonal task, beginning in early spring, as soon as the ground is dry enough. Sods are dug out of long straight ditches and then, after a drying period, piled into little pyramids called footings to enable the sun and air to dry them further. Later the turf is stacked by the roadside; towards the end of the summer it is ready to be brought back to the house, to be stacked neatly by the gable or, even better, in a special turf shed. In a good year without too much rain the turf dries into concentrated efficient fuel. But after a wet summer, you face a winter with smoky, unwilling fires that give off little heat.

This looked like being a good year for turf. Most of the digging was already done, and the men were now busy with the footings. They were working methodically, piling the turf into neat little heaps, eight to ten sods in each, standing in straight lines. Some worked faster than others; some took greater care. The neatest footer of all was a man called Marty MacDonagh, but then he was the kind who always did well in a team situation—it was as if he needed to show that he could do a job better than another man.

It was therefore somewhat surprising to the others that today Marty's work showed none of its usual tidiness. His footings were crooked and uneven, some had even collapsed. And he wasn't keeping up with the others; he was at least twenty footings behind the slowest, who was a young lad doing his very first season on the bog.

One of the front workers, a man called Long John, because he was at least a head taller than any other, made a gesture in Marty's direction and winked at Seamus Lee, the man next to him.

"I'd say Marty has other things but turf on his

mind today."

"And wouldn't I make a bet on what it is?" said Seamus, sniggering.

Marty was far away, but sounds carry on the bog, and he had heard every word they said. He straightened up and looked at them proudly. He was well used to the ribbing from the other men and had an answer ready for each of their comments.

"Well," he said loudly. "Who would be thinking of turf that had a prize-winning mare at home, due for her first-born any minute? Not that any of you would understand," he muttered in conclusion.

That was enough to shut them up. No one was in a position to argue, since all they had ever won was a fifth or sixth prize at a small, local pony show. Marty's Connemara pony consistently took the championship—not only on her own home ground but all over Ireland, even at the Dublin show, beating contestants from every other part of the country, as well as horses of every other breed! This was a feat previously unheard of, and all over Connemara patriotic pride had conquered envy. Everyone shared in Marty's triumph, as if the mare had belonged to them all. And apart from the slagging, which the men simply could not resist, they willingly forgave Marty for the tendency to conceit that had inevitably developed along with his many wins.

"Have you the stable finished yet, Marty?" asked one of the other men.

Marty had pulled down his old stable and was building a new one, twice as large and fitted with all kinds of luxuries to house the mare and her offspring.

"That's just it," Marty sighed. "I haven't. Three weeks I've been waiting for the roofing materials. But there isn't a sign of Malachy."

"He be doing the turf like the rest of us," someone suggested lightly.

"I'll tell you one thing," said a man called Connell O'Donnell, who seemed to specialise in informing people of things they already knew, "Malachy's prices may be cheaper—and he doesn't charge VAT—but when it comes to delivery, he isn't all that reliable."

"Veronica has had to go into the old pigsty," said Marty in an aggrieved voice, as if this was the worst fate that could have befallen his darling.

Colm Keane suddenly woke up. He was a strong and wiry man not afraid of speaking his mind.

"What is she doing in the pigsty?" he de-

manded. "She should be out enjoying the sunshine, like every other God's creature. Are you
afraid she be getting freckles?"

At this the other men laughed. Marty considered saying something scathing about
"being shown the gate" but decided he couldn't
be bothered. The only time Colm had shown his
mare, at Roundstone, he had been sent out of
the ring before the actual judging started. That
was the utmost humiliation—to be told that
your pony was not even fit to be judged.

The work continued in silence, everyone
feeling slightly depressed by the thought of
Marty's gorgeous pony cooped up in the pigsty.
Colm was right, she should be running around
the fields, pleasing the eye of anyone passing,
not be locked away, preserved as in aspic for the
sole purpose of the shows. There was no arguing
that, where feminine beauty was concerned,
there wasn't the like of her the length and
breadth of Ireland. She combined all that was
best in the Connemara breed, the solid strength
passed down by her Celtic ancestors and the
elegance and quality contributed by later in-
fusions of Arab and Thoroughbred blood. It
didn't take an expert to appreciate her bulging
front, her lovely rounded hind quarters, the
straight shapely legs. As to her face...once seen,

it was never forgotten: dark wistful eyes...
large quivering nostrils...ears finely chiselled
as by a master sculptor...

Her coat was a light dappled grey. She had a
flowing mane and tail as white as snow.
Rumour had it that Marty had been spotted in
Moran's Medical Hall in Clifden buying large
supplies of peroxide, but then, surely it was
permissible to help nature along with a creation
that was anyhow so close to perfection.

The pony's name, which might seem far-
fetched by Connemara standards, had been
given her by Marty's elder brother Tommy,
when he was home on holiday from the States.
He had been working for forty years as a bar-
man in Hollywood, of all places, and he spent
every night in the local pubs entertaining old
friends with gossip from the world of the silver
screen, boasting that there wasn't a film star in
the history of Hollywood that he hadn't had the
pleasure to know personally. (That, I would say,
means he's spotted them in the bar, one man
commented behind his back. Or on film, more
likely, said another.)

Anyhow, his all-time favourite was the act-
ress Veronica Lake, famous for her platinum
blonde curtain of hair. At the sight of Marty's
yearling filly, even then a striking young lady

with a long blonde mane and fluttering eyelids, he had exclaimed:

"She looks just like Veronica Lake! You're gonna have to call her Veronica!"

And since that day no one had disputed that Veronica was a most fitting name for what was undoubtedly Ireland's most glamorous pony.

* * *

Long John, who was in the lead with his footings, decided it was time for a break. He straightened up and stretched from top to toe, first backwards, then to the left and to the right. Bog work was hard on your back, especially if the back was as long as his.

Relaxing, he stood for a while looking out over the sun-baked landscape, enjoying the sight. It was scorchingly hot—so hot, in fact, that Long John had to take off his cloth cap for a minute. That did not happen very often. Few people had seen Long John without his cap on.

Down below life seemed to have assumed a quieter pace than normal. A lobster boat chugged slowly out to sea. The cottages looked to be dozing as peacefully as the cattle in the fields. Even the lambs kept still amongst the boulders: fluffy white dots in the distance, looking a bit like the bog-cotton growing around the turf plot.

Then all of a sudden, he felt, rather than saw, a movement somewhere behind him. Long John turned to face the great mountains. There it was, still almost imperceptible, but gradually growing in strength. The supple new grass was bending in a characteristic circular pattern, only about thirty feet across. The bog-cotton swirled in the air above it, like smoke from a chimney on a cold day. The wind reached the little lough in the valley and set off a series of short waves, chasing each other around and around, as if someone had stirred the surface with a whisk.

A broad smile spread across Long John's rugged face. He turned to the others, who were all too busy with the footings to notice what was happening. With thinly veiled pleasure he looked out again, and said:

"If it isn't the cuaifeach."

The *cuaifeach* (pronounced koo-foch) is Irish for a special kind of wind, a whirlwind, in fact, or a mini-tornado, appearing only in Connemara and mainly in late spring or early summer following a period of hot dry weather. There is a simple meteorological explanation for this phenomenon: as the ground becomes overheated, the surface air is set in motion, and the unusual topographical conditions of Connemara then cause the hot air to whirl round.

But the Connemara people themselves favour a different explanation—one that is really much more interesting. According to them, the cuaifeach is a wind stirred up by fairies on the move. Why else would it be so unpredictable, so wicked and so devastating? Most of them will have suffered some destruction at the hand of the cuaifeach. Many seafaring families have lost boats, even friends or relatives, to this ill wind, which, unlike most other ill winds, blows no good at all.

And still—still—there is delight written over all faces when the cuaifeach blows. In spite of the apprehension as to what it will bring in its wake, there is the joy of being invited to witness something which is not really intended for the eyes of ordinary mortals. In a strange way, the cuaifeach fills you with awe.

However, on this occasion there was one face in Connemara that registered neither awe nor delight. Marty MacDonagh, who had been lagging even further behind, shot up from the ground so fast that he nearly fell into the trench. He was as white as a sheet under the sunburn he had acquired that day on the bog.

"The cuaifeach!" he exclaimed, horrified. "Where? Show me—which way is it going?"

A mischievous glint lit the eye of a man called Paddy Pat. His name was Patrick, once only, but according to Connemara custom, the name of his father had been added to his first name to tell him apart from all other men named Patrick, called Paddy. As it happened, his father was Patrick too—but he was known as Pat.

"It seems to me," he said archly, "that it be heading straight for Derrysilla."

Derrysilla was the townland where Marty had his farm.

"Holy Mother of God!" he cried, crossing himself. And then he called out, as if he thought the mare could have heard him: "Veronica! Veronica—I'm coming!"

A second later he was halfway down the hill, leaving a trail of kicked-over footings behind him.

The others sighed and shook their heads, as they bent down to put right the damage.

"Sometimes I wonder," said Colm Keane, sending a worried look after him. "Sometimes I wonder if that mare won't be the end of him altogether."

2

arty was running, running as fast as his short legs would take him. He was a stout man, in his fifties, and not normally given to rushing around—he was more of a thorough, slow-moving character. Now in the heat of the sunny afternoon, he soon found himself panting and sweating profusely. Still nothing in the world could have made him slow down. He was running a race against a formidable opponent: the wicked cuaifeach, out to harm his prized treasure and her, he hoped, as yet unborn progeny.

As he ran, he tried hard not to remember the tales his grandmother had told him about fairies who stole little children, but only the pretty ones, leaving their own ugly changelings in their stead. Would they do the same to a beautiful foal? he asked himself. What if they got there before him and he arrived only to find a hideous donkey-like creature making free of Veronica's udder!

Firmly telling himself that fairies did not exist, except in the head of his grandmother, Marty crossed the road and cut across the fields, which were for once dry and firm, not wet and boggy. The wind pursued him from behind—as he turned round, he could see it moving through the high grass, tossing any loose objects, litter and even an empty bucket, in the air. He knew—he felt it in his bones— that Paddy Pat had been right. The cuaifeach was making straight for Derrysilla. And not only that—it was aiming specifically at the small derelict structure down at the bottom of his long field.

The old pigsty.

At least he had one advantage over the wind: he moved along a straight line, while the cuaifeach had to go round and round in circles. So even if the wind moved faster, it had a longer way to go.

Perhaps he would get there in time, after all.

He had to. He simply had to. The pigsty was a tumbledown shack, its walls crumbling, the thatch on the roof rotten. After the onslaught of the winter's storms, it was now so dilapidated it would collapse if you breathed on it. The cuaifeach would do far more than breathe...the pigsty would collapse...with Veronica and her foal, born or unborn, trapped inside it.

Marty sprinted as he had never sprinted before and never wanted to sprint again. He could feel the wind coming closer, it was breathing down his neck, tearing at the shirt on his back. Thirty feet still to go...twenty...ten.

He reached the shed, reached it a second before the cuaifeach launched an attack on the thatched roof, sending large tufts of it flying. After fumbling with the lock for what seemed to him an eternity, Marty eventually managed to fling the door open.

That was his great mistake.

With a force that knocked him off his feet, the cuaifeach rushed past him, in through the open door. What was left of the rotten thatch was catapulted high up in the air, together with a bunch of broken timber-work. Splinters and beams poured into the shed, over Ireland's most celebrated pony.

"Veronica," Marty whispered, beside himself with anxiety and exhaustion. "My pet, don't be frightened. I'm here with you."

But Veronica didn't hear him. She was

galloping around the field. As the cuaifeach darted in through the door, she had seen her chance of darting out of the dangerous, dark, stinking pigsty.

When Marty finally was able to catch the mare, he himself was more or less recovered, but Veronica appeared to be in a state of shock. The large dark eyes were rolling, she breathed hard and her flanks heaved, covered in lather. Patting and soothing her, Marty looked her over carefully for cuts and bruises. It was then that he discovered the colostrum dripping steadily from her udder.

He knew what that meant: labour was imminent.

There was only one thing to do. He led her gently through the wind, which was still considerable, towards his own cottage, picking up a bale of straw from the hayshed on the way. Veronica had calmed down, she seemed almost resigned, as if she felt that whatever ordeal now lay ahead of her could be no worse than the danger from which she had just escaped.

Bridie MacDonagh, Marty's wife of thirty years, had gone upstairs to admire the spectacle of the cuaifeach from the safety of the bedroom window, when she saw Marty rush past. She wondered what was up, but the scene that lay before her, the big mountains and the bay, rippled by choppy little winds so unlike the normal Atlantic swell, soon blotted out that concern. She sat, as she often did, just gazing out over the landscape, seeing the colours shift under the influence of the wind. Then her mind slowly started to wander back, to happier times, when the children were still young, still at Derrysilla, still in Connemara, still in Ireland.

She was so deep in thought she never heard Marty come in. A few minutes later, strange noises downstairs drew her out on the upstairs landing. What she saw from there defied her wildest imaginings.

"Marty MacDonagh!" she called in a shrill voice. "Whatever do you think you're doing? I'm only after hoovering this place!"

Marty was busy spreading straw over the floor of the kitchen—a floor that in his life-time had graduated from trodden earth to cement to linoleum and now lately—to Bridie's pride: a luxurious fitted carpet from Joyce's in Oughterard.

"It's for Veronica," he mumbled testily, as if that would explain everything.

Only now did Bridie discover the mare standing over by the range, a steaming heap of dung just behind her.

"This, Marty," Bridie began, her voice trembling with anger. "This really is the last straw."

"I know it is," Marty said, exasperated. "My very last bale. I just hope it will do her."

* * *

Ever since she won her first rosette as a yearling—at the Galway show four years earlier—Veronica had been a bone of contention between husband and wife. Bridie, like any sensible woman, resented the money and effort expended on the mare who brought them nothing whatsoever in return, apart from the odd rosette, which might be worth a lot to her husband but meant nothing to her. The prize money was negligible in comparison to the bills from the feed merchant, the vet and the blacksmith. Why Veronica should ever need the attention of a blacksmith Bridie could not begin to understand, as the mare was never ridden or worked. The shoes showed off the perfect angle of her hooves, said Marty, made her move even better. As for the vet—the pony only had to snort for Marty to send out a frantic SOS. She had been injected and vaccinated for illnesses so rare Bridie could not even pronounce them.

What had finally set her dead against the mare was the fact that Marty would not consider selling her. Last year it had come to her knowledge that a man from up country had been turned down after offering three thousand pounds for the pony. THREE THOUSAND POUNDS! Bridie had never seen, let alone handled such a sum in her life. What couldn't she and Marty have done with that money? For a start they could have gone to visit their daughters in Australia, seen the grandchildren they had never yet set eyes upon. Was the mare really more important to him than his own flesh and blood?

When confronted, Marty reluctantly conceded to have Veronica put in foal. Pregnancy might not suit her, he said, some of her valuable condition could be lost, but at least it would give them a top quality foal to sell in the autumn. Then surely Bridie would have nothing to complain about?

But Bridie's antipathy towards the mare was not only due to such practical considerations. In plain terms—though she would have died rather than admitted it—she was desperately jealous of the pony. To see Marty lavish his attentions on another female, four-legged or otherwise, see him treat her with the utmost tenderness and affection, aroused in Bridie a violent longing to have had the same for herself, if not now, so at least once in life, in the days when they were young and just married. Over the years she had resigned herself to the fact that her husband did not have it in him to give what she was yearning for. No wonder then that it hurt her now to see him pouring it out—over an animal!

How was she to know that all his life Marty had longed for someone he could love like that? She had never realised that he was incurably shy of women. Though he had tried as a young man, he could never bring himself to be even remotely romantic. His four daughters he had loved with a dog-like devotion which they had soon learnt to take for granted. No one—least of all the girls themselves—had any idea of Marty's suffering when they all left Connemara to work as nurses and secretaries in Australia. By now they were settled there with families, and the parents only heard from them occasionally.

Veronica had become the substitute for all that he had lost. And she had done him proud. She would never leave him, he'd see to that. Moreover, she accepted his love graciously, fully aware that she needed him just as much as he needed her.

Bridie did not have a clue about this. All she was aware of was a stinging pain each time Marty unwittingly provided further proof that the mare meant more to him than she did. There was the incident last Christmas...Bridie had long needed a new handbag, as the handle of her old one had broken. She had dropped several hints over the weeks leading up to Christmas but had little hope that Marty was actually paying attention. Then came the day for their annual Christmas shopping expedition in Galway: Long John gave them a lift in his car, and then they all went their separate ways. Bridie, tired of the hustle and bustle, had stopped for a cup of tea in a coffee shop in Prospect Hill. From the window there she suddenly spotted Marty coming out of the Leather Shop across the road, carrying a large parcel. The shop-window was full of real leather handbags in different shapes and colours. So he hadn't forgotten! Her heart leapt with joy, and she went straight back to Ryans to buy him the sweater she had just decided was much too expensive.

A few days later, as she vacuumed, she found the parcel hidden under his bed, beautifully gift-wrapped, awaiting Christmas.

Anyone can imagine how Bridie felt when Christmas Day came along and the large parcel from the Leather Shop turned out to contain a new show bridle for Veronica. All she got was a tea towel in a brown paper bag—a special Christmas offer from the Connemara Pony Breeders' Society. It had at least twenty ponies printed all over it.

As for the much too expensive sweater— Marty was delighted with it.

***

Once Marty had lit a roaring big fire in the range and settled Veronica comfortably on a thick bed of straw, it occurred to him that perhaps he ought to check if Bridie was all right. She had withdrawn backwards into the bedroom, a strange look on her face, and had not reappeared.

He opened the closed door to find her in there packing, or rather, throwing her belongings frenziedly into the hard little suitcase that she brought out once a year when she went to stay with her sister who was married to a garda in Ballina.

"Going away?" he asked lightly. "Back to see Maureen?"

"Surely not," said Bridie, tossing in the black felt hat she only wore for funerals. "I'm just after coming back."

"Why then would you be packing?"

Bridie straightened her back and said, not without dignity:

"I'm leaving."

"Leaving? Where are you going?"

"It will have to be the old pigsty. Where else would I go?"

"But you can't—" Marty began, remembering the devastation brought to this edifice by the cuaifeach.

"Anything," Bridie said, slowly and deliberately, "anything at all is better than having to share your house and home with…with a pony."

The last word she spat out as if it would have made her sick to keep it in any longer.

Then she clicked her suitcase shut and walked past him, out of the door. Marty followed her downstairs, intending to explain all about the collapsed roof, when a low moan from Veronica made him forget everything else.

Bridie had the decency to wait by the door while he attended to the mare. But when all was over, she announced that she was going.

He did not hear.

So Bridie left the house where she had lived

for over thirty years, and her husband did not even notice. After all, who would care about the wife walking out when there were much more important matters in hand?

Such as the tiny colt foal standing over by the window, shivering and wet, on spindly, unsteady legs, staring vacantly into space. A wretched, mud-coloured little thing, looking as if he wished he could go back to where he came from.

Marty, of course, did not see him like that. To his eyes, the foal was the most beautiful ever.

* * *

Veronica might have been Ireland's most glamorous pony, but when it came to motherhood, she wasn't great. From the start she decided that the trembling wet little creature she had produced was nothing whatsoever to do with her. Indeed, when he tried to approach her, she put her ears back and snatched at him. As he tried timidly to stretch his neck in the direction of her udder, brimming with the colostrum he needed to survive, she planted a nasty kick right in his face.

Marty was devastated. How could his own darling behave like this? Couldn't she see how

helpless her baby was, how badly he needed her
and her milk? The wilfulness that he had
always encouraged as part of Veronica's proud,
self-assured nature, had suddenly become a
major problem. He patted and coaxed her, but
to no avail. When he tried to steer the foal
towards her, it resisted, already frightened,
wise from painful experience.

Marty felt ready to tear his hair out. He had
no idea what to do. The foal looked as if he was
becoming dehydrated—the pink tongue was
hanging out of his mouth, and he was panting.

In despair he went to look for Bridie and
found her trudging sullenly across the field
with her suitcase, on her way back from the
ruined pigsty. She, too, seemed at a loss what to
do. However, after some urgent pleading from
Marty she agreed to come to his aid, mainly
because it pleased her no end to hear that
Veronica had disgraced herself (showed her
true colours, Bridie thought to herself) and that
Marty was deeply disappointed in her.

"I always felt there was a mean streak in that
mare," she could not resist saying, and Marty,
surprisingly, did not spring to her defence. That
showed how worried he was.

As they came in, they found Veronica standing in front of the range, basking in the warmth,

munching the hay Marty had left out for her. The foal was cowering in the darkest corner, as far away from his mother as he could get. He was breathing raspingly through his open mouth.

Marty produced a bag of raisins from the food cupboard and showed it to Veronica, who pointed her ears towards it. Raisins were her favourite snack.

"Only if you behave yourself," said Marty, putting her head-collar on. Then he lifted one front leg, so that she couldn't kick with the others without falling over. Beginning to realise that she was being outwitted, the mare put her ears back to show her displeasure. But she stood reasonably still. Marty gave her one raisin and told her she could have the whole bag, if she was a good girl.

Then he gave Bridie her instructions. She was to grab the foal from behind and guide him gently towards his mother. That was no problem, the foal being so small and weak. Both Bridie and Marty held their breath, as they saw his neck lengthen and his mouth find its way in under the mare's belly.

Quickly, Marty stuffed a handful of raisins down Veronica's throat to distract her.

Then came the sound: a sound more delight-

ful than the most wonderful music: the
gurgling, slurping noise of the life-saving
colostrum being drawn into the little foal's
empty stomach.

Veronica stood quite still, seemingly resigned to the inevitable, albeit with bad grace.
Marty gave her what remained of the raisins.

"You stay behind him," he ordered his wife.
"See to it that he keeps drinking. There's no
telling when he'll get his next meal."

But he hadn't counted on the vigour that
flowed into the little body with the sudden
stream of nourishment. The foal suddenly felt
that he had had enough of human hands on his
bottom and decided to rid himself of them with
an almighty, two-legged kick.

Bridie was sent sprawling with her feet in
the air.

"So, so," said Marty soothingly to Veronica,
patting her on the neck. "Don't let her upset
you."

And then he turned cheerfully to Bridie:

"He's not as weak as we thought."

Bridie picked herself up and with a dogged
expression grabbed the suitcase which she had
left over by the door.

"This is the end," she said. "I'm going back to
Ballina."

The Wildest Foal in Connemara

3

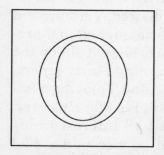

One morning, when Veronica's foal was about two weeks old, the vet stopped off at Derrysilla on his way to Roundstone. He had not heard from Marty for at least a week. With any other client that would have been a sign that all was well: in this case, it was distinctly worrying.

To begin with, there had been frantic telephone calls almost on a daily basis. The mare did not like her foal, would not feed it unless Marty coaxed and pleaded with her, almost to the point of getting down on his knees. The vet suggested that he simply leave her be, let nature take its course. It often took a little while for a mare to get used to her first foal.

The next day Marty was back on the line: It didn't work, the foal wasn't getting enough, just a few drops, then she pushed him away. The vet's suggestion to get another mare, one that had lost her own foal, to feed this one, did not go down very well. He then advised Marty to try and feed the foal himself from a baby bottle.

A further distress call followed: Veronica did not like being milked. The vet sighed and arranged for a milk substitute to be sent out on the bus to Cashel. The next morning Marty reported that the foal was doing grand, enjoying a full stomach for the first time in his life. However, in consequence he had lost all interest in his inhospitable mother, and so her udder had swelled up "somewhat terrible." Could it be mastitis?

Probably not, said the vet, but look out for further signs of infection. Since then there had been only silence. The vet had got increasingly concerned. Now that he had a non-urgent call in the same direction, he had decided to call in to see for himself how his new patient was getting on.

He rather liked Marty, liked him for his kindness and the way he cared for his animals. His attachment to the mare was certainly exaggerated, but then one could well understand why the pony was so precious to him. She has given me the only success I ever had, Marty had confided in him on one occasion. Before I had her I was nothing. Now I am Veronica's owner.

When Marty got too carried away, the vet tried to bring him back to his senses. Personally he was not all that keen on the lady in question. Spending as much time as he did on treating and curing and saving farm animals that had an important function to fulfil, he had little sympathy for those of his patients that fell into the category of pure luxury goods. There was a number of ponies in Connemara kept for the sole purpose of winning rosettes: locked away in stables, force fed, stuffed with supplements, only to be paraded occasionally around a show ring. There was no question of them actually doing something—jumping a course or running a race. Oh no, they were just led around, and then some judge determined the ranking-line, which was usually based on the animals' condition—that is, the amount of flesh they had managed to put on with maximum fodder rations and a minimum of exercise. It was a sort of misguided beauty contest.

The vet couldn't understand it at all—but then, he wasn't a Connemara man. He found it equally hard to accept the custom at the other end of the scale, where pony owners left their animals out on rough common land to fend for themselves without any care or attention. There were still herds of ponies roaming the hills of Connemara, animals whose experience of human contact was restricted to the occasions when they were brought to the stallion or inspected for registration. How they survived was a mystery.

The people in Connemara, tolerant as they were of outsiders, laughed good-humouredly whenever he gave vent to these views. It was strange, in the circumstances, that Marty thought so much of the vet. When it came to Veronica's welfare, he would not accept advice from anyone else, but he took great notice of anything this man suggested. He said himself that the vet was the only person in Connemara that he trusted not to have ulterior motives where his mare was concerned.

It was the vet who had finally persuaded him to have Veronica put in foal, thinking, as he did, that it was high time the mare was put to some use. What if she loses condition? Marty had fretted. She'll soon pick it up again, the vet reassured him. If you have been entrusted with such a superior specimen, it is your duty to see that her genes are passed on.

It hadn't worked out very well, the vet reflected as he drove down the narrow road to

Derrysilla. It was all Marty's fault, of course. If you bring up a creature—any creature—to think that all she owes to life is to look good, it's bound to misfire. Here he was now, with a prima donna on his hands that could not even be bothered to feed her own offspring.

He parked his car and got out, stopping for a moment to breathe in the strong, salty sea air. Marty's cottage was at the end of a long track, out on a headland, with only fields, or rather, rocky bogland, between it and the sea. The place was exceedingly peaceful—much too peaceful, the vet concluded. There was no sign of either Marty or his ponies. But there was smoke coming out of the chimney, on this balmy hot day.

After the vet had knocked on the door and entered, it took him no more than a few seconds to establish that things were not at all as they should. As his eye swept quickly around the kitchen, he was filled with a feeling of mounting dismay.

First of all there was the stench. It was one thing if a stable smelt of manure, that was only natural, but it was not what you expected when you opened the door of a respectable cottage. Then there was the mess—not only from the animals, but from household rubbish, dirty dishes, food going bad. Bridie who always took such pride in keeping her kitchen clean! He remembered how she had showed off the new fitted carpet to him. Where was she now?

Three inhabitants dwelt in the kitchen, each a pitiful sight. Veronica, the glamorous champion mare, stood listlessly by the window looking out, ears petulantly pointing backwards. Her coat, normally so shiny you looked for your reflection in it, was matt and dull. She had lost so much weight that, for the first time ever, the vet could see the shape of her frame.

Even sadder was the doleful figure of the foal cowering in the dark nook under the stairs. A puny, mouse-coloured thing with a head much too big hanging lethargically.

But worst of all was the sight of Marty sitting by the kitchen table. In his hand was a half-eaten piece of bread and jam which he was sharing with three bluebottles. His face, drawn and sallow, had at least three days' growth of beard on it. The shirt he was wearing was smeared with unmentionable stains. Bridie who always looked after her husband so well! What had happened to her?

"Are you all right, Marty?" was the only thing the vet could think of saying. He was quite overcome by this picture of accumulated unhealth.

"He suckled for one and a half minutes at sunrise..." Marty mumbled. "Then he had another few drops, not so long ago... But Veronica is put out, because I've run out of raisins..."

"Marty," said the vet, in what he intended as a friendly, yet authoritative tone, "your ponies need help. I know exactly what's good for them. Will you let me do as I please?"

Marty looked at him and blinked, only now realising who it was that had entered the cottage.

"What do they need?"

"Fresh air, surely," said the vet.

The pallor on Marty's face intensified.

"But the cuaifeach..." he protested weakly. "What about the cuaifeach?"

"Who?" said the vet, never having heard of this phenomenon.

"The fairy-wind," Marty explained. "They were after Veronica's foal. I think he may be a changeling—that's why she won't let him suckle."

"Nonsense," said the vet, putting on Veronica's head-collar. "There's no wind blowing today. Now tell me in which field you want them."

"Down by the sea," said Marty meekly,

suddenly relieved at having the responsibility taken off his shoulders. "My best field with the iron gates...I had it prepared for them."

The vet led Veronica down the path to the sea, the foal and Marty following. It pleased him to see that the mare had perked up the minute she got out of the cottage. So had Marty, for that matter, and even the foal was scuttling along quite happily. He pushed open the heavy cast iron gates—Marty's pride, presumably pilfered from the ruins of some abandoned big house in the area. Then he let the mare into the field. The foal followed.

For a minute or so he and Marty watched them in silence. It was a nice field, comparatively smooth and well drained, with lush, health-giving grass benefiting from the closeness of the sea and lots of wild flowers. Veronica sniffed at the grasses, the buttercups and clover and then took herself off at a gallop around the field. Here and there she jumped high in the air, bucking exuberantly. The foal kept up as well as he could, the spindly legs going like drumsticks.

Gradually the anxiety on Marty's face lifted. At first he worried that they might hurt themselves, but the vet assured him they wouldn't. Round and round they went, racing each other as if they were going for the Galway Plate. Each time they passed the gate, Veronica threw Marty a reproachful glance, as if she thought he might have let her have this fun sooner.

"Do you think," he asked the vet after a while, "that it may have been bored they were?"

The vet nodded.

"There is nothing as unhealthy as boredom for a Connemara pony."

After a while Veronica slowed down. She drew breath for a moment and then put her head down to sample the fragrant grass. The foal, equally hungry after the exertions, confidently approached his mother, as if previous intimidations had been forgotten. Veronica, preoccupied with the grass, took no notice of him. He had a long, good breakfast.

Marty stared. There was a smile on his face, tears in his eyes.

"No such thing as nature," the vet said lightly. "Will you leave them here, so?"

"Anything you say," Marty replied breathlessly. "Anything you say."

"Where is Bridie?" asked the vet as they walked back to the house.

"In Ballina. She wrote to say she won't come back until the ponies are out of the house...I suppose I can write back to her now...once I've cleaned up the kitchen."

"It might be a good idea," the vet suggested gently, "to get a new carpet. Before she comes back."

"I'm sure you're right," said Marty with unexpected enthusiasm. "That's exactly what I'll do. The old one will be just right for Veronica's new stable!"

* * *

For a while things went reasonably well in the MacDonagh household. A new carpet was purchased with some of the money put aside for tickets to Australia—Marty hoped it would be some time before Bridie thought of checking the amount in the blue tea-caddy. Bridie herself returned home, and Veronica, though not exactly revelling in the joys of motherhood, tolerated her son, at least enough to let him eat now and then. Besides, the foal proved to be a precocious one: he soon started to eat the rolled oats Marty put out for his mother. She turned up her nose at all her old favourites now that she had unlimited supplies of fresh meadow grass. She had begun to develop a matronly grass belly which Marty found most unbecoming. If only he had had her new stable ready! But Malachy still had not turned up with the materials—by now he was presumably at hay.

Bridie seemed quite pleased to be back. No further mention was made of the ponies' sojourn in the house, and she took greater care than usual preparing good meals for Marty.

"I'm glad to see you back," he said to her one evening in a for him rare display of affection.

"Well now," said Bridie, who wasn't very demonstrative herself. "I had to come back, didn't I? I mean, if nothing else for the potatoes."

Marty turned away and said no more. However was he going to tell Bridie about the potatoes?

To people in Connemara, as all over Ireland, the potato—that is, the proper, home-grown potato—is almost a sacred thing. That is perhaps not so strange, when you consider that in the old days, people depended on it for their survival. Just think of the millions of Irish people who died in the last century, when the potato was struck by blight. But history is not the only reason why this food is so highly appreciated: anyone who has ever tasted a real Connemara potato, coming straight out of the black turfy soil of a lazybed enriched with seaweed, can confirm that there are few delicacies in this world comparable to it.

In spite of a long life together, Marty and Bridie did not have many things in common. However, one thing they did share: their love of potatoes, and the dedication that went into the work of growing them. Together they dug the long, narrow beds, marked out with string to get them absolutely dead straight. Together they brought panniers of seaweed up from the shore, they conferred for weeks about the different varieties and carefully selected the seeds. These were then ceremoniously put in, the first by St Patrick's Day, weather permitting. Now and then in the weeks that followed they would take a stroll down to the potato garden to see how the shoots were coming along. It was a great pleasure to see the plants grow. But no pleasure could be greater than the lifting of the first crop, sampling the tender fruits of their labour, softly boiled and swimming in rich yellow butter.

What Bridie did not yet know was that this year there would be no potato crop. The sowing had been done as usual, in fact with extra care, and with thirty extra seed potatoes put in for good measure. What they had not taken into account, however, was the presence of a certain young creature, who for every day was showing new signs of developing into the wildest foal in

Connemara.

For ten days now, Marty had been making attempts to catch him. He wasn't really used to foals, but the vet had told him that it was important to get a colt caught and handled at an early stage, before he got too obstreperous. This one was already obstreperous enough, so it was high time.

The task was not made any easier by the irritating habit Veronica had lately acquired of running away in the opposite direction the minute she saw her owner approach. It must be that the sudden freedom had gone to her head— after all, she had been confined to a stable ever since she was a year old.

The foal, heartily approving of this new game, had responded by inventing a whole range of evasive measures, such as galloping around him in circles until Marty felt dizzy, turning right round and galloping straight into the sea, splashing water all over Marty as he tried to save him from certain drowning, charging at him till it was Marty who ran for cover, or if all else failed, getting up on his hind legs and challenging him to a real stallions' fight.

Eventually Marty realised that he must resort to his own superior mental powers, if he was ever to get the better of this foal. He

therefore lured him into a small hollow at the
corner of the field and blocked the only way out.
Or so Marty thought. The foal, who seemed to
have an answer to everything, simply jumped
the stone wall which—disaster and devastation—separated the field from the potato garden.

The long, narrow lazybeds, firm from the dry
weather, softened by the tender greenery,
proved to be ideal runways for a hyperactive
foal. Marty watched, horrified and powerless,
as the delicate plants, with their tubers at the
most sensitive stage of early growth, in a matter
of minutes were trampled into a slimy black
pulp.

What would happen when Bridie found out
did not bear even thinking about.

4

he weather broke eventually, and a few stormy weeks followed. The materials for the stable arrived, but the wind was too strong to do any roofing. Marty fretted about his ponies being out in the bad weather, but there was really nothing he could do about it.

One dull and misty Sunday morning, he went down to feed them—or rather the foal, as Veronica still refused to eat anything but fresh, succulent grass. Her son, on the other hand, gladly gobbled up her rations.

Bridie was preparing to go to Mass, dressing herself in the smart new outfit she had bought in Galway during the week. Marty strongly suspected that the Australia kitty had again been raided—where else would she have got the money? He hadn't had a chance to check the amount in the tin under her bed and did not dare broach the subject, in case it brought her attention to the missing carpet money. They had solemnly promised each other never to take money out of the kitty, only put it in.

He had still not managed to catch the foal— or Veronica, for that matter, but that did not worry him to the same extent. Her figure was more of a problem—she had always been plump, as a good show pony should be, but the fat had been in the right places. Now it all seemed to have gone to her stomach. Her hind quarters had never picked up what they lost when the foal was new-born, and her withers no longer had that cushioned softness that judges used to admire. Marty thought to himself that if he had known that foaling would have this effect on her, he would never have let her go through with it. On the other hand, it might have something to do with her temporary change of diet and life-style. If he could only get that stable finished...

One concern weighing heavily on his mind was the rapid approach of the show season. In one way or another he would have to have them both ready for showing by the middle of July, or the Connemara shows would be denied their own star attraction.

How this was to be achieved in a matter of weeks Marty honestly did not know. Veronica he could probably get into shape soon enough once he got her into shelter...but the brat—that was a different thing altogether. Because he was never still, he seemed to use up every scrap of the good food he was given—no matter how much he ate, he only grew taller and lankier, without an ounce of fat on his bones. The head was still at least two sizes too big for his body, and the ugly mousy colour persisted. If only Veronica could have been shown without him— but that wasn't permitted: the rules clearly stated that a mare must be shown either barren or with her foal at foot.

The priority, however, was to have him caught, preferably without a struggle. The vet had offered some advice based on sound horse psychology: "Don't chase after him, make him come to you. Never tower over him, go down low, and you'll appear less threatening. Reward him each time he approaches you."

Marty did not trust his colt enough to "go down low" in front of him—that would most likely have resulted in being trampled black and blue. But he saw the sense in the vet's recommendations and decided to try out the method this morning with the safe barrier of the cast iron gate between them. The foal, having seen the black bucket in his hand, was already jumping up and down excitedly.

This time Marty did not open the gate to put the bucket in but took a handful of the rolled oats, crouched down low and stuck his hand in between the thick iron bars. The foal contemplated the food for a while and then carefully came up to take it, stretching his neck long.

Poor little fellow, Marty thought to himself. He believes I will kick and bite him, like his mother. It's all that wicked mare's fault.

He held out another handful, and this time the foal came closer...and closer again. By the time the bucket was empty, he was standing up against the gate munching happily from Marty's hands, although he recoiled each time Marty tried to lay a hand on him.

When it came to giving him his daily apple, Marty had a brilliant inspiration. He cut the apple into four pieces and placed one piece between his own teeth. Then, crouching even lower, he stuck his head through the gap between the iron bars. The foal stared at him, not knowing what to make of this new game. He sniffed at the apple but did not quite dare take it.

To make it easier for him, Marty pushed his head a little further in. The foal reflected for a while, then found himself irresistibly drawn to the mouth-watering titbit in Marty's mouth. He took it gingerly between his four baby front teeth and chewed eagerly before coming back for more. The other pieces were taken in the same way, each with more confidence. Finally he started to lick the remaining apple juice from Marty's lips and chin. The rough tongue and the tiny little whiskers tickled Marty and made him giggle.

"You're not such a bad little lad after all," he said affectionately.

But when the razor-sharp new incisors got hold of his earlobe and delightedly started to nibble at it—perhaps he thought it was a teat?—Marty made a sudden, defensive jerk. It must have been then that something went wrong. For when he tried to pull his head out, he found he couldn't move. He was firmly stuck between the bars of the gate, at a spot some eighteen inches off the ground.

The foal was at his ear again, trying to suck milk out of it. Marty gave him a smack on the nose, harder than he had intended, for it resulted in another wild gallop—just what he wanted to discourage.

Every attempt he made to move was in vain. He was fastened as securely as in a vice.

"God Almighty," he sighed. "And me thinking I was getting along so well!"

He spent a long time lying in the wet grass, soaked to the skin by the pouring rain, thinking of better ways to spend a Sunday morning. Both ponies had come up and were standing over him, watching him intently, slightly concerned. It would have been an ideal opportunity to catch them both.

Everything was very still, as it often is in Connemara on soft wet mornings with little wind. The air was mild and smelled of damp summer grass. Far away the sound of the church-bell mingled with the bleating of lambs. If Marty hadn't been quite so uncomfortable, he would have enjoyed the peace.

It was shattered briefly when Bridie appeared in her new finery, hopping mad, giving out to him for ruining his best suit and making them late for Mass.

"Get up at once!" she had commanded.

"Oh I would," Marty moaned miserably. "I would—if only I could!"

Bridie got on her bicycle and pedalled off to church, muttering something about not knowing what to expect next. Anyhow, that little disturbance was nothing compared to what followed later. Once Mass was over, Bridie returned with half the population of Cashel, some hoping to be of help but most only there to gape at the sight so vividly described to them by Bridie outside the church.

"What's he doing, Mam?" asked one child.

"How did he get there?" another wanted to know.

"Why won't he get up?" demanded a third.

They talked about him as if he wasn't there.

"What I can't for me life work out," said Paddy Pat, "is why he can't get his head out when he was able to get it in."

"If you ask me," said Connell O'Donnell thoughtfully, "his head will hardly have grown any bigger since this morning."

"Looking at him," said Seamus Lee, "you'd think he had his head on the block. All that's missing is the executioner."

Marty's cheeks burnt with indignation.

The men went off to his shed for tools that could set him free. The children, in the meantime, turned their attention to the ponies that were hovering in the background, curious but at the same time intimidated by so many people invading their land.

"How small he is," they said about the foal.

"Much smaller than Colm Keane's filly. And what a funny colour."

"Is it true he's a changeling?"

"Veronica isn't half as pretty as she was last year. Look at her big fat tummy."

The men reappeared, armed with the complete contents of the shed: a loy, spade, hay-fork, pick-axe, iron bar, sledge-hammer —even an old oar that Marty had found washed up on his land after a storm. Each man proceeded to apply his own piece of equipment on the basis of his personal theory as to how it would do the job. There was a frightful racket of shouting and laughing and clanking, as the arsenal of tools was put to work.

"Mind the gate," Marty pleaded. "And don't be scaring the ponies."

"Perhaps you'd rather we went away and left you?" Colm Keane snapped. He was in a bad mood, because he was missing the roast his wife had prepared for dinner. After that Marty kept his mouth shut. He shut his eyes, too, expecting at any moment that a heavy instrument would accidentally land on his head. He couldn't decide whether he was disappointed or relieved when the men finally gave up their efforts. But the bright idea then conceived by Paddy Pat turned out to be an even worse alternative: He

would go over to Owen's and ask him to bring
the lorry along. Then they'd take the gate off its
hinges and send it down to the metalworks in
Carna.

"What about me?" Marty wondered.

"You'll have to go too. With the gate, on the
back of the lorry."

"All the way to Carna? On a Sunday?" Marty
wailed. "How could I make such a spectacle of
meself?"

"There's no other way," said Colm Keane
dismissively. "Unless you want to stay here."

The others drifted off for their belated
Sunday dinners, promising to look out for
Owen's lorry and come back to help lift Marty
and the gate onto the platform. Bridie stayed
with her husband. She offered to get him something to eat, but he declined. The thought of his
forthcoming trip to Carna had robbed him of all
appetite.

"Just tell me one thing," said Bridie. "How on
earth could you get yourself into such a
position?"

Marty explained.

"Couldn't I have sworn," his wife exclaimed,
"that it was the dratted foal what was
behind—"

Here her speech was interrupted by a

sudden, piercing scream.

Bridie was not a woman given to screaming for no good reason, so at first Marty thought something dreadful had happened to her. He tried to turn his gaze in her direction but could only see her feet, where they stood in a pair of new brown shoes on a little hillock behind him. Then, in the dead silence that followed, it dawned upon him that only one thing could have provoked such a strong reaction in her: from the hillock she had the potato garden in full view.

"There was one thing now that I forgot to tell you," he said hurriedly. "When you were away, Connell's sheep got into the garden. I had to chase them out. Twice."

"Is that so?" Bridie replied, her voice laden with doubt.

"At least six of them. He's a bad one, Connell, for letting them stray. Only the other day I saw them way over by..."

Bridie wasn't listening. She had taken herself off into the garden to inspect the damage. When she came back, Marty was seized by a sudden fear that she might attack him, kick him with the new stout shoes or, perhaps, hit him over the head. He felt very vulnerable where he lay.

But Bridie just slumped down on a boulder next to him.

"I shall have to congratulate Connell," she said grimly, "on having such very special sheep. They leave hoofprints and pony dung behind. He ought to sell them to a circus."

There was another ominous silence. Marty, knowing that this was not the end of the matter, braced himself against what was to come next.

"The foal will have to go," Bridie said eventually.

Marty noted with relief that she sounded utterly weary rather than angry.

"Sure now," he agreed willingly. "I be selling him as soon as the show season is over. It'll only be a few weeks."

"He's got the curse on him," Bridie muttered.

"He has all right," Marty said eagerly, just to please her. "To tell you the truth, I can't wait to get rid of him."

A little later they heard noises up on the road. It was the men coming back, led by Long John who was carrying a large heavy object.

"Marty, you're saved!" they called. "Long John's come up with the solution!"

This materialised as the jack from his car. They only just managed to fit it in between the bars.

A few minutes later, Marty scrambled to his feet, very wet and very stiff, but apart from that none the worse for his ordeal.

He was met by a huge cheer from the crowd.

At this the foal took fright, jumped the nearest wall and ran away, as far as it could get from the commotion.

It took the men the rest of the afternoon to herd him home.

As for catching him, that wasn't even worth trying.

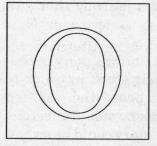ne major event in the Connemara calendar is the annual Connemara Pony Show in Clifden. On show day this small town, always popular with tourists, becomes jam-packed with visitors and traders, farmers and holiday-makers. From early morning onwards the two streets that make up most of the town brim with strollers and motor-cars. Shops and stalls do a roaring trade, while a steady stream moves towards the showground at the bottom end of the town. There you can enjoy music by traditional fiddlers, see set-dancing by little girls in Celtic costume and admire prize-winning samples of Aran knits, home-made cakes and organically grown lettuces.

But the overwhelming attraction of the show is the ponies. Here, hundreds of Connemaras brought from all over Ireland are paraded, judged and given awards. Spectators and buyers from all over the world flock around the show ring to see real Connemara ponies at their best. For some of the animals exhibited, Clifden could be the first stage of a journey that will take them as far away as America or New Zealand.

And this is where Connemara's pony breeders bring the cream of their stock in order to take on—and sometimes beat—the well-fed contestants from the prosperous limestone lands further east. What victory could be sweeter than that won against a privileged adversary? No wonder the Connemara man takes such pride in his ponies. They are his vindication, living proof that the lush grass and rich soil of other areas do not necessarily produce the best end result.

Much will be forgiven the Connemara resident who takes home the Clifden Championship.

The late summer usually marks the beginning of a wet season in the West of Ireland. Thus it often rains on show day, and many visitors go home with a gloomy grey picture of the little coastal town that spends much of the year bathed in sunlight. This year was no except-ion—during the night before the show the heavens opened for a downpour, the like of which had not been seen for years. People woke up to flooded hotel rooms, gardens turned into lakes, and various forms of structural damage. It was the sort of challenging situation that occurs from time to time in Connemara and keeps the population from getting bored.

There were floods all along the main road from Galway to Clifden, and the bridge on the south side of the town was under two feet of water. That, however, did little to stop the flow of horse-laden vehicles bound for the show. The variety was great: from converted sheep-trailers and ramshackle cattle trucks (usually approaching along minor roads from the north and south) to smart Range Rovers and the latest in bionic horse transport design (usually arriving on the main road from the east).

The simplest, most flexible method of transport was no doubt the one used by a man from Recess: he drove his own small car along the road, while his mare followed it cross-country. Now and then she stopped and put her head down to graze; then he opened the car window and whistled, whereupon she took up the pursuit once more. She skilfully kept to the higher ground and sniffed carefully when she came to a flooded patch to determine the depth of the water: tricks the Connemaras learn out on the mountains. Only once did she actually get lost—but that wasn't really her fault. Passing a farm where a stallion was kept, she wrongly assumed that this was where she was heading for and turned in, full of joyful anticipation. Surprised at the unfriendly reception she encountered—the stallion keeper was just trying to load his treasure to go to the show—she quickly realised her mistake and soon caught up with her owner again.

Quite a few exhibitors walking their ponies to the show had to lead them across the flooded bridge. Some people waded straight through— they had been on their way since the early hours of the morning and could hardly get any wetter than they were already. Others mounted their animals and rode them bareback through the worst. A few walked near enough dry-shod on the parapet, while the intrepid ponies slopped through the water that reached well over their hocks and knees.

However, the worst problem awaited the pony owners when they arrived: the Owenglin river that normally flows gently at the bottom of the showground had burst its banks and was now overflowing into the main show ring, drenching the grass where the ponies were to show the best of their paces. Would the show still go on? The first class was just about due to start, and the rain was still falling heavily. The water level in the showground was rising by the minute.

Naturally the show went on. A few drops of rain had never yet stopped it, not in its sixty-odd years of existence.

And so the spectators shivered in the rain, while soaking wet ponies splashed through the giant puddle of the ring. At least they were all competing on the same terms, equally un-flattering to everyone. There were the yearling colts, yearling fillies, then the two-, three- and four-year-olds and after them the stallions, paraded round and round, lined up, trotted up individually in front of the judges, lined up once more and finally awarded their prizes.

Those local men who were not showing ponies of their own were as always glued to the ringside, watching eagerly to see who was showing what and who was winning what over whom. But during the long-drawn-out judging sessions, they turned to each other to exchange comments about the ponies shown, displaying a knowledge that was almost uncanny.

"Hasn't Josie's filly come on great this year?"

"She still doesn't move. It's that sprain she got the first winter, she's suffering from it all the time."

"Seal's Rock can't have had much to eat last winter."

"Sean only gives him one bucket a day. Too lazy to do him properly."

"That colt has good bone."

"Strong in the head, though. Like a horse."

To most people the word "pony" means a small animal, to be played with and ridden by children. That is not so in Connemara, where the breed called Connemara Pony epitomises all that is best in the equine world. Specimens of this breed can often attain the size of a horse, but anything "horsey" in looks or manners is frowned upon. To Connemara people, as to *connoisseurs* all over the world, the well-defined beauty and character of a typical Connemara pony constitutes the ideal.

One topic of conversation that cropped up now and then was whether Marty MacDonagh would turn up with Veronica for the five- and six-year-old mare class in the afternoon. So far he had not arrived, but they all felt that he could not possibly fail to bring the reigning champion. Still, at Ballyconneely, Claddaghduff and Roundstone, the three smaller local shows that

preceded Clifden, there had been no sign of
Marty, even though Veronica was entered in
the show catalogue. The men from Cashel now
found themselves approached by others who
were anxious to know how things were at
Derrysilla.

"Is it true that the mare is after losing her
condition? They say the foal is a sorry sight. No
bigger than a donkey foal—and no more hand-
some."

"I hear she's a terrible rearer," one man said
about Veronica. By that he did not mean that
she had a tendency to get up on her hind legs, as
might be suspected, but rather, in Connemara
terms, that she was not too keen to feed her
young.

"It is Marty who has her spoilt," said another
disapprovingly. "She is so spoilt I shouldn't
wonder if he doesn't chew the hay before he
feeds it to her."

"There's life enough in the little fellow," one
of the Cashel men pointed out.

"Life!" someone repeated. "I would say so.
Ask Peter Conneely!"

Everyone knew what the foal had done to
Peter Conneely's hay. He had jumped out of his
field for the umpteenth time, into the
neighbour's hay-meadow, where he found him-

self facing a row of neat haycocks, lovingly made the day before by Peter and all his relations who had come over from England specially for the hay-making. Whether he was taking the line that attack is better than defence, or simply thought the haycocks presented more fun than danger, the foal busied himself for hours in the field, until one of the English relations discovered what he was up to. By the time the offender was removed, only shreds of the haycocks remained. A wet day it was, too, so the hay that had been trampled into the mud was beyond saving.

"He's a bit wild, that foal," Connell O'Donnell informed them, his tone suggesting that he was the first person ever to make that reflection.

"So would you be, if you were born under the cuaifeach," said Paddy Pat.

The others groaned.

"Stop! Haven't we heard enough of the cuaifeach?"

They had all been subjected to every detail of Veronica's foaling —some of them three or four times.

Their speculations about Marty's attendance at the show were now at an end, because the class for five- and six-year-old mares was announced. The ropes at the entrance were removed, and there, appearing from nowhere, was Veronica with her foal, led round by Marty, as usual the first to enter. The mare looked the same as ever, prancing along proudly, showing herself off. She was familiar with the Clifden show. It was the scene of her greatest triumphs.

Marty had made it in time for the class only by the skin of his teeth. It had never occurred to him that the foal would not follow its mother into the trailer. And Veronica was never a problem to load—she couldn't wait to get going once she had her tail bandage and her travelling boots on. But the foal had no intention of going anywhere near the trailer. He galloped in circles around it, until even Veronica got restive and wanted to back out.

Eventually, half an hour before the class was due, the foal must have got hungry—or rather, thirsty, for he suddenly climbed the ramp and stuck his head in to suckle. Quick as lightning Marty raised the ramp, tipping the surprised foal in next to his mother. He peeped in to check that the foal was standing on his feet, not his head, and then they set off as fast as they dared through the floods, with Long John driving.

The other contestants were beginning to fill the ring. With each sodden, bedraggled-looking entry Marty felt a little happier. It was the

Clifden Show, and he was once more walking around the ring with the best-looking mare in Ireland by his side. Round and round they went, Veronica naturally, indisputably, assuming a leading position, as if the contest was already settled.

She looked magnificent. Three weeks in the new—finished—stable with loads of hard feed and daily grooming sessions had worked wonders. Her figure was more or less restored, movement and presence were unimpaired. Her grey dappled coat, shampooed and gloss-conditioned, shone like burnished silver. Whiskers, ears and feathers had been trimmed to perfection, the flowing white blonde mane and tail did not have a hair out of place, and the shapely hooves were oiled jet black. She was dressed in the expensive brass and leather bridle he had bought her for Christmas. She was the best turned-out pony in the ring—and she knew it.

Pity about the foal...Marty had given him an extra sprinkling with holy water before entering the ring—he could do with the help from above. There was no way he could have improved on nature in his case, since he could not even get near the little brute. Even so, no beauty treatment in the world could have made the head smaller, or the body more mature. Possibly if the coat had been dyed a different colour...Marty noticed there was mud on his hind legs and wished, for the sake of his own reputation, that he had at least been able to brush him down. On the other hand, the mud was so close to his coat in colour that it hardly showed.

One thing Marty had to concede was that the foal was remarkably well-behaved. It might be that he was intimidated by the crowd, for he remained meekly at his mother's side, kept pace with her and was generally unobtrusive— which was the best that could have happened, all things considered.

Veronica, too, had a surprise in store, but then she often did come up with some strange quirk once she found herself in a show ring— presumably the idea was to attract everyone's attention. Today's caprice was a sudden surge of motherly devotion: she kept turning her head back with tender glances at her baby, making low whickering noises to reassure him—all very fetching. It struck Marty that, if only she had behaved like that since the day he was born, it would have saved them all a lot of trouble. It was obvious that some love and understanding was all the little fellow needed to make him behave himself.

He caught the eye of one of the judges and thought he saw a wink. It was a judge who had awarded Veronica several of her championships in different venues over the years. And sure enough, the steward made a sign to Marty to take up the first place in the preliminary lineup. He willingly obliged. Veronica blew herself up in an imposing square stance, and the foal helpfully stuck his big head under her belly, where no one could see it.

Marty couldn't help chuckling to himself when, out of the corner of his eye, he saw Colm Keane and a couple of other contestants being shown the gate. So much for Colm's overgrown filly foal. Now there were only eight mares left in the ring, five with foals, all of them ponies that Veronica had beaten on numerous occasions in the past.

The show was a walk-over.

He held the championship in his hand.

The preliminary number two was selected: a stocky dun mare from the east coast, in splendid condition as might be expected, but somewhat short of leg, Marty thought critically, for such a gross body. She, too, had a colt foal, equally dun, equally dumpy. While the judges decided on the other rankings, that foal got bored and came over to introduce himself to his neighbour.

Veronica's foal, who had never met anyone his own size and age before, immediately got interested. The two foals sniffed each other earnestly and then, suddenly, got up on their hind legs, pretending to fight. The crowd, also bored by the lengthy judging process, smiled benignly at the little ones at play.

Then the colts decided to have a race down the long side of the ring. As they splashed through the water, Marty sent out a prayer that the foal would return before Veronica noticed. She looked so good when she stood stock still, her neck slightly arched, head cocked and ears pointing forward—just the way the judges liked to see her.

But Veronica was already looking anxiously behind her to the left and to the right, sending out trembling whinnies for her darling. When she could see no sign of him, she suddenly threw herself in the air, swivelled round and set off in pursuit, splattering mud all over her spotless coat.

Marty was taken completely by surprise, unused as he was to such displays of maternal affection. The lead-rope slipped through his fingers and he found himself ignominiously darting to and fro trying to catch his own mare. Isn't it typical? he muttered to himself. She hasn't as much as looked at him since the day he was born—and today of all days, she has to go into hysterics over him!

Veronica was chasing frantically around the ring, whinnying loudly, so blinded by concern that she didn't realise she had passed her foal and that he was now running after her, in response to her distress calls. The dun mare had also stomped off after her son, but her owner had at least managed to keep his hold on the rein and was galloping along next to her. The other foals were also running around excitedly, and in consequence, so were the mares— with or without owners attached to them. The stewards did what they could to shoo each foal back to its respective mother, but no one was quite sure who belonged where, so the confusion only got worse. Before long the whole show ring was in pandemonium.

"Pardon me," said a spectator in a thick foreign accent, turned to the Connemara men who were watching the spectacle with considerable glee. "Can you tell me what is going on?"

"Sure now," said Paddy Pat, his blue eyes glittering. "You'd do well to wonder about those goings-on."

Seamus Lee was not late to chip in:
"It is the cuaifeach."
At this the others roared with laughter. Well said, they ho-hoed, slapping Seamus on the back. The cuaifeach! Very well said!

The visitor, nonplussed, scanned the ring, as if hoping to discover whatever was so amusing.

The dun mare, with all her bulk, soon started puffing and blowing and could be led back to her place. Her foal, having lost track of his new friend, followed obediently. One by one the other mares were brought back under control. The only two unaccounted for were Veronica and her foal, who were still going flat out around the ring. To the onlookers it was uncertain who was chasing whom—and why.

The vet was right, after all, Marty groaned inwardly. Two buckets of oats a day really is too much for them.

He had given up the useless attempts to catch the mare, as they only served to excite her further and besides made him look an absolute fool. So he stood still, waiting for her energy to flag, which had to happen eventually, however many oats she had guzzled. But before it came to that, the foal suddenly stopped in his tracks, made an unexpected U-turn, caught sight of his mother and bolted towards her.

For a moment they looked set for a head-on collision. Everyone watched with bated breath. But then Veronica—give her her due—realized the danger and slammed on the brakes. Unfortunately, the speed at which she was going and the slippery wet surface did not allow for such sudden halts. She skidded on all four feet and collapsed in a heap right in front of her offspring.

A few giant sloppy strides over the slushy ground brought Marty to her side, just as the mare dazedly scrambled to her feet. He grabbed the filthy wet lead-rope, which had been brand new for the day, and then quickly, and with relief, satisfied himself that she wasn't injured.

The three of them resumed their exalted position at the top of the line, all covered in mud. Veronica hardly had the appearance of a potential champion any more, but then, neither had any of the others. There were some scowls and angry glances directed at Marty and his ponies who had been the cause of all the commotion.

The judges reappeared from the little hut in the middle where they had taken refuge while the tumult went on and hastily got the remaining ponies into some kind of order. Then it was Marty's turn to bring Veronica up for inspection. As usual they looked admiringly at her impressive build, paying scant attention to the foal, and asked him to trot her up. But after only a few strides they stopped him.

"The mare is lame," they said. "She must have hurt herself in the fall. You had better show her to a vet."

Marty stared at them as if he didn't understand English.

"She's disqualified," the female judge said gently.

The steward made a gesture towards the gate. The gate! Only now did the penny drop. He was being shown the gate. He, Marty. And Veronica! The most beautiful pony in Ireland.

"Sorry Marty," said the judge who, he thought, had winked at him before. "Hard luck."

He walked out, his gaze firmly fixed on the ground in front of him. Veronica resisted and did not want to go, she was waiting for her prize, and the ovations. He had to pull her out by force. Never in his life had he felt so humiliated.

His friends were at the ringside but he did not see them.

"Well done, Cuaifeach!" called one of them to a bout of raucous laughter.

And that was how the foal got his name. A

fitting name, to be sure, and one that was to follow him to the end of his days.

6

t was one of the first days of September, and a crisp northerly breeze had swept in over the country, bringing cool clear weather of the kind that makes autumn quite an attractive prospect, especially after a humid late summer. Now the sunlight had returned with a new brilliance—the grey mountain tops rose darkly against a blue sky flecked with white clouds, the amber frill of seaweed along the low tide mark shone brightly against the deep blue sea. While the bogs were beginning to fade into their restful buff-coloured winter robe, the hillsides blazed with yellow furze and purple heather. Fuchsia and late honeysuckle blossomed outside the cottages.

People in Connemara were taking their first breaths of autumn air, drinking in the freshness, the new earthy smells, whiffs of turf smoke on the air. After a summer that had not been bad, weather and harvests considered, they could now settle down contentedly to a season of less hard work, more leisure and relaxation.

But there was one man in Connemara who was less than content with his season. He was sitting on a rock, high up on a hillock overlooking his land, and he was sunk in gloom. His summer had been a disaster. Everything had gone wrong, and now it was all over. There was nothing in the world he could do to put it right.

Down by the shore he could see the little foal playing in the shallow water of the low tide, splashing with his hooves, then jumping in the air and landing squarely with all four hooves plunging into the water at the same time. His mother meanwhile was grazing quietly, keeping a safe distance.

Watching the cause of all his misery, Marty still could not find it in his heart to dislike the exuberant little fellow. Even the nickname, given and used with scorn, he had affectionately adopted. A right little cuaifeach he was—no name could have suited him better.

The previous Sunday he had taken his ponies to the Oughterard Show. Determined not to have a repeat performance of the spectacle in Clifden, he had devoted the best part of ten days to training his foal for show ring behaviour. By applying all the cunning he possessed, he had first of all got him caught. Once that was done, Cuaifeach became surprisingly manageable. Clever as he was, he probably realised that Marty now had the upper hand, or else it had dawned upon him that being handled had its rewards—such as large, green apples. Only occasionally, at the end of a long training session, he would get fractious and rear up or sink his sharp little teeth into his master's flesh. But on the whole, he made good progress.

Bridie complained bitterly, as all Marty's chores were left unattended and she had to do her husband's work as well as her own, while he, as she termed it, "played with his ponies." Marty explained to her that the family's honour was at stake. After the fiasco at Clifden—from which Veronica's fetlock had mercifully recovered—he simply had to get things right for Oughterard.

"You wouldn't want me to be the laughing-stock of the country now, would you?" he pleaded with his wife.

But a laughing-stock was exactly what he had turned out to be.

The jeering started the minute they entered the ring. To ensure that Cuaifeach performed properly, Marty had got Long John to come along and lead the foal just behind himself and Veronica. This had taken some persuasion— Long John simply couldn't see the point. Foals were not normally led in Connemara, they were just left to run along with their mothers. Only when Marty vowed that he was the only man strong enough to manage the little brute, did his friend grudgingly agree.

But what was so funny about it? Funny enough for the bystanders to howl with laughter. Marty, of course, could not possibly see how comical their little foursome appeared to the spectators: first his own squat figure, accompanied by the sumptuous, glamorous Veronica, almost swamping him with her confident, pompous stride. This was certainly a sight familiar to many of the show visitors, but they were not prepared for that which followed: the tailpiece of the equipage, headed by Long John's huge, towering frame, crowned, in honour of the day, by a pink woollen hat that looked more like a tea-cosy. And in his hand...in his hand was a rope, attached to a tiny, mud-coloured foal, stomping along furiously, with the most disagreeable expression that anyone had ever seen on an animal. People couldn't help laughing. And poor Marty couldn't for his life figure out why.

"Hey, Long John!" they called. "There's a bug stuck at the end of your string!"

Renewed hoots of laughter.

And then...the nightmare continued. Mickey Coyne was called in to take up the leading position. Mickey Coyne, whose moth-eaten grey mare Veronica had beaten easily— in Corrandulla, in Spiddal, in...in every show that counted. Year after year after year! And before he was over that shock, another mare, one he did not even recognise, was brought in as number two. Marty felt faint. Finally it was his turn. By then Veronica was disenchanted at having been passed over twice and did her best to have a swipe at the two mares in front of her. Cuaifeach loyally kicked at their foals, and Long John needed all his strength to control him.

Perhaps these bad manners were the reason why the judges moved them down even further, to fourth place after the individual inspection. They did concede that Veronica still looked splendid but mumbled something about the foal being "on the small side."

So it was Cuaifeach's fault, after all. He was

the direct cause of all this summer's misfort-
une. Why deny it? Bridie was right—the foal
had the curse on him.

Marty sighed. He sighed often these days.

Suddenly the bird-song, the sleepy buzzing
of late insects was disturbed by the jarring
noise of a motor. Looking up, Marty saw a smart
new car towing an expensive horse-trailer
coming along the narrow road leading to his
cottage. It stopped and parked by a clump of
trees, where no one could see it, except Marty
from his high vantage-point. A door slammed,
and a man continued along the road on foot.

Marty soon figured out what this was all
about. Someone was coming to see him, intent
on taking an animal away, but equally intent
that Marty should not know exactly how intent
he was. It was an old trick amongst livestock
dealers.

He wondered fleetingly who his visitor could
be. No one local—he knew their cars as well as
he knew their faces, and none of them possessed
such a good trailer. Besides, none of them would
stoop to this type of subterfuge.

He had no intention of going down to find out.
He was in no mood to see anyone. It was much
nicer to sit here on his hillock, look out over the
sea, watch a heron fish, seals diving off a rock

and, far out, a curragh being rowed in the direction of the oyster-beds.

Of all places to be depressed in, his native one was not the worst.

When Bridie brought the visitor along to see him a little later, his reaction was one of annoyance. And his irritation grew when he saw who the visitor was: a certain Mr Greene, whom he had met many times before and liked a little less each time.

It was Mr Greene who had offered him three thousand pounds for Veronica the year before. In a way Marty had been relieved that the offer came from him and not from someone more sympathetic, for in that case, he might—just might—have felt tempted to consider it. Three thousand pounds was an awful lot of money. But no money in the world would have induced him to hand over Veronica to this man. He was one of those types from up country who dealt heavily in ponies, yet, for reasons of his own, would not admit to it. Instead he professed that, beside his regular office job, Connemara ponies were his all-abiding interest in life. Behind his back it was said that money interested him much more than ponies: his work somehow brought him in touch with foreign buyers, to whom he could sell the ponies at hugely inflated

international market rates. His own supply
came from small farmers such as Marty, who
had no access to the foreign customers and so
had to be grateful for whatever money Mr
Greene and his likes offered them. Occasionally
this man would fork out a big prize for a proven
winner—just so he could cement his own cred-
ibility and prestige, show that Ireland's best
ponies all belonged to him. On the strength of
that he would then deal in any old rubbish at top
prices—or so wicked tongues had it.

For a long time he had been after Veronica,
continuously upping his bids. But he was not
going to have her. Over my dead body, Marty
thought. And it occurred to him that he ought to
write his will, giving clear instructions as to
exactly what should happen to the mare if he
died. He didn't trust Bridie when it came to big
money.

As a matter of fact it wasn't Veronica Mr
Greene had come for this time. Marty might
have guessed as much from the broad smile of
relief covering Bridie's face.

"Mr Greene is taking Cuaifeach," she
announced, beaming all over.

Marty could have kicked her. She must know
by now that, whatever your own feelings, you
never ever let on to a buyer that you were keen,

even prepared to sell. It weakened your bargaining position. The buyer should be the one to
plead, twist your arm, beg on his knees, in-
crease his offer time after time, until you eventually, reluctantly, agreed to possibly consider
selling, naturally to a higher price. Here was
Bridie talking as if the deal was already done.

"And he'll give us fifty pounds for him," she
added, in a delighted tone suggesting that she
would gladly have paid Mr Greene the same for
ridding them of the little beast. Actually, she
would have. Only the other day, when Cuaifeach had pulled all her clean laundry off the
line and rolled on it, she had declared her
intention of drawing her secret savings from
her Post Office account to pay someone to take
the dratted foal away.

But she shouldn't have let that on to Mr
Greene. He was obviously determined to buy, or
he wouldn't have brought his trailer. For once
Marty had had the upper hand in the negotiations, and he could have got a decent price for the
foal.

If Bridie hadn't gone and ruined it all.

"You go and make some tea," he told her. "I'll
bring Mr Greene back in a minute."

The two men watched her go, and then Mr
Greene turned to Marty.

"I was sorry to see you doing so badly in Oughterard," he started in his drawling voice.

Marty glared at him without getting up, taking in his natty appearance, the pin-striped suit, a gleaming white shirt and a red polka-dot bow-tie. The thin grey hair had been draped carefully over a large bald patch. The well-polished black shoes, Marty noted with pleasure, had been placed in a boggy spot and would start letting in water at any minute.

"Fourth is not so bad," he muttered. "The class was big."

"But Veronica is worth more than the other three put together," Mr Greene averred. "I told you as much last year. There is nothing to compare with her the length and breadth of Ireland."

"You tell that to the judges," said Marty sullenly, unsure where the other man was aiming.

"It's that foal," Mr Greene stated, lifting the silver-fitted measuring-stick for horses that he always carried and pointing it in the direction of Cuaifeach, who was just having a quick spot of lunch. "You shouldn't let him suckle her, you know. He's just draining her of strength and beauty."

Marty said nothing.

"I had a word with the judges at Oughter-ard," Mr Greene continued. "They all thought it such a shame...but they simply couldn't award a mare with a misfit like that at foot. Besides, he has taken a lot out of her."

"Well there's nothing much I can do about it," said Marty despondently.

"You must get rid of the foal," said Mr Greene, "and the sooner the better. With him gone, you can at least start building her up again for next year's season. If you don't, you'll never get her back into the top ranks again."

"Why do you want to buy him?" Marty asked suspiciously. "If he is such a...misfit?"

Mr Greene laughed deprecatingly.

"You never know...he may grow...the grass is richer in my part of the country...He could possibly make a nice little riding pony if he is gelded...I'm taking a chance, of course...his temperament doesn't seem to be all that good. He may well turn out to be worthless."

Marty watched him doubtfully. Something in this speech did not ring true.

"So I couldn't offer you very much for him," Mr Greene resumed. "Fifty pounds is as high as I'm prepared to go. Let's cut out the bargaining, for once. There's nothing like a straight deal."

"Sorry now," said Marty slowly. "But if his

mother is worth three thousand, fifty pounds seems a little on the low side to me."

"The knacker won't even give you that," Mr Greene replied cold-heartedly.

Marty went white. Those words gave voice to fears that he had been trying to push from his mind all summer.

"You have to be realistic," said Mr Greene, now in a more reasonable tone. "He will never be approved as a stallion. You'd be hard pushed to find a buyer for a gelding—even if he looked and behaved better. That only leaves the fair— that is, the slaughter-house—and me. Now will you take my fifty pounds—or would you rather see him eaten as steak in France?"

Seeing that this approach had struck home, Mr Greene now softened his tune further.

"That foal isn't really good enough to bring on," he said. "But I'm willing to have a go, because I happen to think the world of his mother. And I believe in good blood. It may come out eventually."

By now it was obvious that Marty was wavering.

"I'll tell you this," said Mr Greene gently, "you'll be saving yourself a lot of trouble by getting rid of him now. Why not take the easy option, Marty? Give him to me—and you'll have the money into the bargain."

Fifty pounds would just about cover the cost of Peter Conneely's ruined hay harvest. Where else would that money come from? Peter was getting insistent.

"All right," he sighed. "Shall I take him over to your trailer? I seen it over in the trees."

"I'll take him myself," said Mr Greene, grinning broadly. He counted out five ten-pound notes and pressed them into Marty's hand.

"I should give you something for luck..." Marty said.

"Don't worry," said Mr Greene. "Some other time."

A little later, with Veronica shut in the stable with an extra bucket of oats and a recalcitrant Cuaifeach on his way towards the trailer, Marty climbed his hillock once more to see that the foal loaded without trouble. He had had plenty of training leading up to the Oughterard Show, but you never knew...

He reached the top just in time to see the first attempt. Cuaifeach put his head down to sniff the ramp, looked cautiously inside and then sniffed the ramp again. That was fine—it was how an intelligent pony reassured himself before entering an unknown space. It didn't mean he was going to refuse—on the contrary.

But Mr Greene couldn't have had much experience of intelligent ponies, or else, he just didn't have the patience, for while Cuaifeach was standing there innocently sniffing the trailer, Mr Greene's stick landed on his backside with an almighty blow.

The foal swung around in an instant to face his attacker. Next Marty heard a shrill yelp echoing across the fields—whether it emanated from man or beast was hard to tell. Before he had time even to reflect on it, he found himself rushing down the hillside towards the trailer, as fast as he possibly could.

When he arrived at the scene, he could hardly believe his eyes. There was Cuaifeach tied to a tree, and Mr Greene beating him furiously over the head with his stick. The foal, demented with fear, sweating and rolling his eyes, was rearing up, trying to defend himself with his front legs. But the rope was tied so short he could hardly move at all.

"Stop!" Marty roared. "Will you stop it!"

Mr Greene turned towards him, red-faced with anger. Now Marty saw that, while his right hand held the stick, the left one was wrapped in a large white handkerchief stained with red.

"You blooming eejit," he snarled at Mr Greene. "What have you done to him?"

"He bit me," the other man whined, clutching the hand in the handkerchief. "The beast, I believe he's taken a finger off me!"

Trembling, he removed the bandage. All fingers were intact and the bleeding had nearly stopped, but there was a splendid row of marks from sharp little incisors—such as Marty had already seen on various parts of his own anatomy.

With Mr Greene still stunned by the intervention, Marty quickly untied the foal that was quivering from head to toe. Poor little pet, Marty thought. He had never known anything but kindness in his life, it had taken so long to convince him that he had nothing to fear from humans. Cuaifeach buried his head against Marty's chest, as if he wanted to seek consolation and reproach him at the same time, and Marty stroked him very gently to calm him down. The little body was hot and clammy under his hands.

When the foal's breathing became more even and the trembling had nearly stopped, Marty turned to lead him back to his field. Then Mr Greene woke up—until then he had only stared at them, open-mouthed.

"What do you think you're doing? That's my pony!"

"The deal's off," said Marty curtly, walking right past him.

Mr Greene came running after him.

"You can't do this!" he wailed. "It was an agreed transaction. The pony is my property. You have no right to take it back."

"Surely you don't want a pony that takes your fingers off," said Marty in an attempt to be reasonable.

"I don't care what he does! He's mine, and he's coming with me!"

He tried to grab the lead-rope from Marty's hand, and for a moment they grappled over it. Then Cuaifeach, alert to the danger represented by the other man, took a flying leap and butted Mr Greene in the back. A ram couldn't have done it better —the man tumbled forward. Unfortunately for him—though Marty and Cuaifeach probably thought otherwise—there was a large ditch right in his path. He fell headlong into it.

"Sorry now," said Marty. "I forgot to give you this."

He threw the fifty pounds towards the figure spread-eagled at the bottom of the ditch. Then he quickly walked on with the foal, while Mr

Greene got to his feet, furiously brushing the black slush off his shirt front, only making it worse.

"You'll regret this!" he shouted after the two retreating figures. "Believe you me, you'll live to regret it!"

Veronica, having finished her extra feed, now suddenly missed her darling and was calling anxiously from the stable. She didn't have to wait long—Cuaifeach was soon back with her.

With them in the stable was Marty.

He felt as if he never wanted to part with either of them again.

Besides, he wasn't too keen to go in and face Bridie.

Out of Sight

7

 laying around in the sea had always been one of Cuaifeach's favourite pastimes, but at the end of September there came a day when the wild little foal had more than his fill of watersports.

Dawn broke on this day just as on any other day at Derrysilla, the only unusual thing being an exceptionally high tide. As the water began to ebb, scores of seagulls gathered along the shore in search of special treats for breakfast. Reflections of the rising sun glowed on newly formed rock pools. Cuaifeach and his mother feasted on the short grass on the foreshore, which had been drenched and seasoned by the salt water.

Little did they know that this was the last day that the foal was ever to spend grazing by his mother's side. It was also the last day for a long time that he was to see his devoted breeder. In fact—over the next two years he was to see very few human faces at all.

But as yet the little foal grazed happily by his mother's side in the pink light of daybreak on a fine September morning in Derrysilla.

* * *

Things had never been worse in the MacDonagh household. The only reason Bridie was still there was that her brother-in-law, the garda in Ballina, had relatives from New York over on holiday, and they were using the spare room, so there was no room for her in her sister's house. Since the episode with Mr Greene, Bridie no longer spoke to her husband. When he tried to address her, she simply walked away, so he had had no chance to explain to her exactly why that deal had fallen through. She went to bed early, locking the bedroom door, and Marty had to sleep on the settle bed in the kitchen. In despair he had taken to going to the pub every night, where he had too many pints of beer, whilst complaining to his friends about life's wretchedness in general.

No one in Cashel was surprised to learn that

Cuaifeach had managed to drive a deep wedge between husband and wife. As Seamus Lee put it:

"The marriage was about the only thing left for him to wreck."

Every time Bridie went to the shop cum post office cum pub for her messages, she launched into a new jeremiad about the foal's latest depredations: if he hadn't eaten her begonias, he had trampled her strawberries or chased the ducks so they wouldn't lay. It was a generally accepted fact that Cuaifeach, like the wind that named him, brought a trail of devastation in his wake, and there was a genuine sense of sympathy for the MacDonaghs. In the end Paddy Pat came up with a solution—perhaps not permanent, but still long term. A cousin of his was married to a man from Ervallagh who had recently inherited grazing on one of the islands in the bay. The island was long since uninhabited but had plenty of good grass. Other farmers grazed sheep there, but Peadar King, the cousin's husband, planned to put his own colt foal out for the winter—"to mature out of harm's reach," as he put it. Now he was looking for another animal, colt or gelding or donkey, to keep it company.

The offer was heaven-sent. Marty could

hardly believe it. Paddy Pat gave him a lift over, and the two men shook hands and decided to bring the two colts out on the morning of the big September tide, when the ebb was at its lowest and the distance across to the island some hundred yards shorter than at high tide. Peadar lived at the end of a headland and kept his boat, a curragh, in a harbour nearby. As he went fishing whenever the weather permitted, he would be able to check on the animals every now and then through the winter. It was an ideal arrangement.

And this was the day. Marty got up early and cooked himself a hearty breakfast—it was a long time since he had someone to cater for him. As Bridie came down to make herself a cup of tea, he thought he detected a glint of curiosity in her eye—as if she guessed something was afoot and would have liked to ask what. But he did not volunteer any information—that would be delivered after the event. A little tea-time surprise for her.

When Marty went down to the field to collect his ponies, they were both reluctant to leave the delicious moist grass, but Veronica perked up when he took her to the stable—she probably thought there was another, late show coming up. However, once it dawned upon her that her foal was not coming in with her, she set up a terrible racket, whinnying loudly and plaintively. She had, at the eleventh hour, just when it was least desired, forged a strong bond of affection with her son.

Leading an obstreperous foal is a difficult task at the best of times. With its mother hysterically calling it back, it is near enough impossible. Getting Cuaifeach to walk along the road was about as hard work, Marty thought, as pushing a heavily laden turf-cart up a steep track—without the donkey in front. And it was not as if he had any time to lose—in the interest of safety, Peadar had said, the crossing had to be done while the tide was way out. Another low tide would not come up until mid-November, and by then the weather would have turned, and the water would be cold.

As he struggled along, Marty did not think kindly of Long John's mother-in-law, who had had to fix her appointment at the Regional Hospital for today of all days. If it hadn't been for that, they would have been driving along in comfort now, with Cuaifeach in the trailer behind them, and there would have been no need for this back-breaking exercise.

Up on the main road, a late tourist stopped his car and jumped out to take photographs of the labouring, sweating Marty and his foal.

"You going far?" he asked in halting English.

"Another seven miles," Marty told him.

The tourist shook his head.

"In my country we use trailer for horse. Much better. Saves time."

Marty shrugged.

"Time means nothing to a Connemara pony."

As the foal got out of hearing range of his mother, he started to move at a more reasonable pace, and the walk became more of a pleasure. The autumn sun shone brightly among tufts of grey cloud, there was a bit of a cold breeze but no more than to ripple the surface of the sea. People were out on the foreshore with buckets picking winkles and clocheens. With some luck Bridie would be doing the same. Both of them enjoyed their clocheens, the small scallops living in the bay. And there would be cause for a celebration this evening. The end of their problems...

He passed the narrow causeway leading to Inishnee and took off to the right, up the ancient track running along the foot of the massive Errisbeg mountain. The track, rarely used nowadays, was stony and overgrown, and the foal started jogging excitedly, so that Marty himself had to break into a trot to keep up with him. This was no less exhausting than dragging him along, so after a moment's consideration, he held in the eager colt and took off the lead-rope.

Mercifully, Cuaifeach did not bolt towards the horizon but, slightly unsure in his new freedom, preferred the safe proximity of his companion. In this way they walked pleasantly together side by side, all the way to Roundstone. There the rope came back on again, and they went by the back way of the village across to Ervallagh, arriving at Peadar's cottage five minutes before the appointed time.

Peadar was already there, waiting with his pony. He was a thin, sinewy, somewhat gruff man with thick black hair and bushy eyebrows. As always on seeing new ponies, the men quickly sized up each other's. Peadar's colt was bigger than Cuaifeach and steel grey. He had a weak front to him and huge hind quarters that rose at least four inches higher than the withers. Marty thought it made him look like one of the kangaroos on the girls' postcards from Australia.

Peadar, on his part, eyed Cuaifeach up and down as if he were something the cat had brought in.

"Who is he by?" he asked, scowling.

"Jackie's horse," Marty replied, not without pride. "The one that used to win in Clifden."

Peadar shook his head and spat.

"That one should never have been allowed to breed."

Marty held back a sharp retort about kangaroos—this was not the right moment to fall out with the man on whose help he depended. Instead he nodded towards the grey colt.

"What's his name?"

"Name?" Peadar sneered. "Ponies don't get names till they're registered. At two," he added, as if Marty didn't know.

Then he made a gesture towards the curragh left far down at the low water's edge.

"It's time we went."

He had brought two long blue ropes, and with these they made halters for the colts. On Peadar's scornful recommendation, Cuaifeach's smart leather head-collar—specially acquired for the Oughterard Show—was left under a stone, out of reach of the salt water. Then they put the halters on the foals and led them over the slippery black stones and seaweed, which usually lay at the bottom of the sea.

As they climbed into the boat, Peadar left Marty to hold the ropes, while he himself took the oars. The two colts stood squarely on the foreshore watching and wondering what was about to happen. Marty wondered too—he had no experience of this sort of thing and hoped that Peadar was as confident as he made out.

"Hold steady now," Peadar called, shoving the boat off land by a mighty push with the oar.

The ropes stretched. The foals did not budge. The boat continued to move out. Marty held on as he had been told, stood up in the stern so that he could lean forward and pull.

"Sit down, you eejit!" Peadar bellowed, a fraction too late. The fragile curragh—only a wooden frame covered in tarred canvas—was already rocking alarmingly, and as Cuaifeach made a sudden jerk, Marty lost his balance and fell clumsily onto the gunwale. The boat keeled over on its side, pitching him into the water. He was closely followed by Peadar, who had also been off-balance, leaning on his oar and pushing.

It was still shallow, which was fortunate, as neither man could swim. Peadar, cursing, took a few strides to catch his boat just before it sailed off on the tide. In the confusion, Marty had lost his hold on the ropes, and Cuaifeach, quick as ever to take advantage, galloped straight back the way he had come, followed by the grey colt. They passed Peadar's cottage and disappeared out of sight.

"Blow it!" Marty cried. "He be going back to his mother in Derrysilla!"

As it happened, the attraction of Veronica's apron-strings had been forgotten in the joy of having a new friend. While Peadar held on to the curragh, Marty went to look for the ponies and found them playing together in a nearby field—if playing was the word. It was more a case of Cuaifeach bullying the other one, chasing him around in circles.

By the time the men were ready for their second attempt, the tide was already turning. Peadar curtly told Marty to take the oars, while he himself drove the delinquents knee deep into the water from behind. As he overtook them, Cuaifeach, now in his most jocular mood, splashed heartily with his front hooves, sending cascades of water over Peadar, as if he wasn't wet enough already. The man cursed again and, with a firm hold on the ropes, jumped into the curragh, pushing it out as he did so. Surprised by the sudden movement, the colts followed, and once they reached deep water, they had no option but to swim. Peadar now sat in the stern, holding the ropes, calling out directions to Marty for the nearest route to the island.

"Are you sure they're all right?" the latter asked anxiously.

All he could see was four ears and two noses bobbing up and down among the short choppy waves.

"Nothing we can do if they're not," said the other man unsympathetically, muttering, "in a cold wind like this, you could do without being soaked to the skin."

His spirits were about as low as the tidal water.

Then, with a malicious tinge to his voice, he told Marty about the fellow who had swum a mare over to Blue Island earlier in the year.

"Stone dead she was when he got there. Drownded. Couldn't swim."

"I thought they could all swim," Marty protested. "If I had known..."

Peadar grimly shook his head.

"You only know once you arrive."

Marty rowed and rowed, as if his life—and indeed Cuaifeach's—depended on it. He got red in the face and hot in spite of the biting wind. When they finally landed on the beach of the island, he was dead beat but delighted to see Cuaifeach rise from the waves. He, too, was tired, but otherwise none the worse for the unusual exercise. But now the most difficult part remained—saying good-bye to him, for goodness knew how long. The little foal that he had helped into this world, whose very existence he himself was responsible for. Every day of his life he had had Marty to care for him. What awaited him now?

A quick look around the island revealed that it was quite large, some hundred acres, with good grazing, fed by the seaweed and the white calciferous sand from the beaches. The old ruins would provide shelter against the winter storms, rushes and bracken would offer soft beds, and there was plenty of fresh water. Marty told himself this was all a pony needed. It was he who was over-fussy.

The two men, shivering in their damp clothes, put out to sea again. This time Peadar did the rowing. Marty sat in the stern looking back towards the island. Cuaifeach and the grey colt were standing high up on a rock, looking at the boat—forlornly, it seemed to him. He felt a stab in his heart and a burning sensation under his eyelids. It had started to rain, and the drops ran down his cheeks like tears. Was it the rain? Just in case it wasn't, Marty kept his face turned away from Peadar.

But as the image of the foals gradually faded against a thick grey cloud, so Marty's heartache subsided. In its place came quite a different sensation, which he at first guiltily rejected but then, as the foals merged into the horizon, happily embraced.

A feeling of immense relief.

He had got rid of Cuaifeach!

* * *

When Marty walked into his kitchen that afternoon, still light-headed with the success of his achievement, he found Bridie cleaning clocheens by the sink.

"Cuaifeach's gone," he announced smilingly.

"About time too," she replied, which wasn't a very nice answer, but it pleased Marty no end, for it was the first time she had uttered anything at all to him in almost a month.

Then she added:

"There's a letter for you."

Marty eagerly seized the envelope. This was indeed his day. It must be from one of the girls; no one else ever wrote to him.

But the letter did not bear an Australian stamp. It was a white, official-looking envelope, postmarked in Dublin, with his name and address formally typed on it.

Marty didn't like the look of it at all. Such

letters seldom held good news.

Still, nothing could have prepared him for what it actually did contain. It was from a Dublin firm of solicitors, saying they represented Mr Greene. Mr Greene was taking him, Marty, to court, alleging that he had reneged on an agreed transaction over a pony. In consequence Mr Greene had suffered substantial losses, and moreover, while attempting to stop Marty taking the foal away, he had been assaulted and injured. On two different charges he was now seeking damages amounting to two thousand nine hundred and fifty pounds—or assets worth the same.

Even if Marty found it hard to follow the convoluted presentation of the case, the word "damages" and the amount stood out clear enough.

Mr Greene was trying to get nearly three thousand pounds out of him, and judging by the tone of the letter, he had some rightful claim to it.

Where would he find that amount of money? The kitty did not have a penny in it, all that money had gone towards paying Peter Conneely for his ruined hay. Cuaifeach again! Anyway, that had been only fifty pounds.

Assets worth the same...he had no assets.

Only the farm...if the judge ruled against him, would he have to leave his house and home? Give up his livelihood?

Oh no. Wait a minute.

There was another asset.

Mr Greene knew exactly what he was doing.

Marty would have to give him Veronica.

8

fter Cuaifeach's pamper-
ed start in life, it must
have been quite a change
suddenly to find himself dumped on a deserted
island, cut off from the close link with his
mother, which had in the end become warm and
loving, and from the care and concern lavished
on him by Marty. Still, he can't have been too
unhappy there, for he thrived and grew well: by
the end of the first winter he had attained a
decent size for a yearling, with plenty of bone
and reasonable proportions, and when his new
summer coat came through, it was no longer
mousy in colour, but a rich, glistening bay.
These were all signs that he was well suited to
his environment; perhaps the healthy natural
life-style appealed to the wild side of his nature.
It certainly became no less wild in the two years

he spent on the island.

It was, in fact, not a bad place for a tough young Connemara pony. There was much to see and watch, both on the mainland, which was clearly visible in good weather, and on the water, where on calm days boats went to and fro, lifting lobster-pots and servicing the fish farms. On stormy days the sea in turmoil presented a fascinating spectacle.

On the island itself, nothing was ever the same from one day to the next. Being so close to the elements meant a constant process of adjustment for the creatures that lived there. The two ponies roamed from one end to the other, following the dictates of weather and seasons. There was the rocky storm beach exposed to the west, where delicious fresh seaweed, especially the tender sweet dulse, was flushed up after each gale. There were the sandy coves on the eastern side, perfect for luxurious rolls. The island had a criss-cross pattern of smooth grassy tracks—the old "streets," where the ponies could stretch their legs in a flat out gallop. Inland, raised rocks and hillocks provided convenient look-out posts with views in all directions, and in between were hollows softened by fern, screened by thick furze. Springs poured out unlimited supplies of fresh drinking water, and the formerly well-tended fields were covered in sweet grass and dotted with clover and daisies.

The two colts shared these facilities with a number of other inhabitants. For, although the island had long since been abandoned by humans—or perhaps one should say, because it had been—it abounded with animal life. The two new arrivals were soon accepted by the rest of the population. Horses are, after all, peaceful creatures with few enemies. By nature gregarious, they are known to strike up friendships with other species, and it was not long before some rather unlikely forms of camaraderie developed.

The animals on the island came in all shapes and sizes. Tiny sand-hoppers bounced around the ponies' noses as they dug into heaps of stranded seaweed. The rocky shores were home to numerous birds: oyster-catchers, rock pipits, little terns, ringed plover. To begin with, these were, understandably, alarmed by the presence of the ponies—the plover, especially, staged screaming displays to distract them from their nests. But they, too, soon learnt that they needn't go to such lengths to protect their offspring from the huge animals with the hard hooves. It was actually amazing how rarely it happened that one of them accidentally trod on an egg.

The other small animals—mice, rabbits and stoats—liked to keep close to the ponies on cold winter nights, if nothing else for the warmth their big bodies gave off. Although the little ones kept themselves well hidden under stones and in holes, the sheltered spots selected by the colts during the worst gales were likely to become quite overcrowded. On sunny summer evenings, Cuaifeach occasionally indulged in a spot of rabbit-chasing—he probably missed Bridie's ducks, the fun they had had together. The rabbits seemed to enjoy it, too. For one thing, they knew he could never catch up with them—whenever he came uncomfortably close, they simply darted into a hole. A minute or so later they were back, sitting boldly right in front of his nose, as if begging for another game.

The sea offered a range of interesting acquaintances: a dolphin sometimes came into the bay on the east side, where he jumped high, greatly impressing the ponies. On the rocks just off the island was a large colony of seals. For a long time they stared warily at the newcomers and kept well away from the island's shores. But when spring came and the ponies took to playing in the sea, the seals threw caution aside and came swimming up for a closer inspection—brave, probably, in the knowledge that, in this element, they had the upper hand. Whenever Cuaifeach saw them approach, he would swim out to join them. They waited in the water, stock still, but the minute he reached them, they dived out of sight. Disappointed, he turned back to the shore, only to find that the seals had resurfaced in a different spot and were now waiting for him there. The game went on for as long as the pony could take it—the seals seemed to get more pleasure out of it than he did.

The one creature that Cuaifeach became truly attached to was, funnily enough, a large dog otter. He did not live on the island—he must have had a holt on the mainland nearby—but he was a frequent visitor. The otter liked the colt just as much: each time, as soon as he arrived, he came to seek him out. From the initial mutual respect, an increasing familiarity developed between them. They rarely played together, but they liked to do things jointly: Cuaifeach grazed while the otter ate his fish, they took turns to roll in the sand, went for runs or swims and then rested side by side. It was one of those rare kinships based on sympathy alone: they had little in common, but still liked being together.

Peadar's colt took no part in these rather odd friendships that Cuaifeach seemed to specialise in. He preferred to stay with the flock of sheep grazing quietly in the fields further inland. Cuaifeach had little time for sheep—except for scattering them now and then. And he got bored with the other colt, who so willingly allowed himself to be dominated. From the very first day at Ervallagh, when Cuaifeach had chased him around the field, he had followed him round submissively. This sometimes irritated Cuaifeach, and he ran off, away from him. However, at times the two colts got on quite well, especially when they were able to have some good crack together, like on those few occasions when humans landed on the island.

The sight of a human being evoked strong feelings in Cuaifeach, stirred some deep memory—the memory of Marty, most likely, for he was, after all, the human with whom he had had most contact. And with this memory must have come some kind of longing—a longing for all that Marty had given him, all that he had since had to do without: human care, human attention, human love. And it must have been this longing—undefined in his tiny pony-brain but pulsating strongly in his big heart—that drove him to such extremes of behaviour when-

ever his gaze fell upon an unsuspecting human
visitor.

There were two quite different types of two-
legged callers to the island. One kind they could
almost have done without: the local fishermen
who put in for their tea and took no notice of the
ponies whatsoever. Peadar King also fell into
this category, though he actually took the
trouble to check them over each time. But he
never touched them, never spoke to them. And
if they tried to cheer him up by running off and
inviting him to come after them, he merely
shrugged and went back to his boat. He was a
dead loss.

Better then was the other kind, which, like
the migratory birds, arrived only in the
summer season and then only on days when the
sun shone and the sea was nice and settled.
Their calls were eagerly awaited and hugely
enjoyed by the ponies.

They were the holiday-makers.

From them the colts drew enough adulation
to see them through the bleak lonely winter.
And they made absolutely sure they got it. The
moment they heard or saw a boat approaching,
they mounted a high cliff overlooking the
harbour on the north side. From there they
were most conspicuous, and it wasn't long be-

fore the inevitable "oohs" and "aahs" broke out as a sign that they had been discovered. They were quite a sight at this stage: well nourished by the mineral-enriched grass of the island and fit from all the exercise there, they were positively bursting with midsummer condition. Their sleek summer coats glowed in the sunshine, and they carried themselves with the pride and self-confidence that are in themselves tokens of good health. This, combined with their long, unkempt manes and tails blowing in the breeze, made them look exceedingly wild and impressive.

A few of the holiday-makers confronted with this view quickly decided to change their plans and visit some different island instead. However, most reached for their cameras and went ashore.

And that's where the fun started. Once the ponies had reassured themselves of the commitment of their audience, they led them a dance across the island, now evading them, now attracting them again. If they noticed that interest in them was flagging, they staged a magnificent stallion fight or something equally spectacular to get the cameras clicking again. In these performances it was always a case of the grey colt acting in a supporting capacity, while Cuaifeach took on the starring role. Veronica would have been proud of him.

One lovely day in July, Johnny Mullen, a Roundstone fisherman, put in at the harbour with his large Galway hooker. With him he had a family of holiday-makers—mother and father, teenage son and daughter, and the daughter's boy-friend, who was on holiday with them. They had a caravan at Gorteen, the large holiday-site on the white beaches at Roundstone, but had got Johnny to leave them out on the island for the day. He was to collect them again at high tide in the evening.

It took a long time to unload their kit. Johnny had never seen so much needless paraphernalia. At least I needn't worry in case the weather breaks, he said to himself. They have enough here to see them through a week.

Just as he was ready to go, he looked up and spotted the two ponies standing as usual up on the cliff. Somehow he suspected that his passengers did not have a lot of time for things like wild horses, but the prospect of having to load everything again...he was already half an hour late for the fishing-trip he'd promised the hotel...

So he said nothing. Just as well the others hadn't noticed.

Guided by some mischievous instinct, the ponies withdrew to the inner parts of the island and kept out of sight while the family installed themselves comfortably in a beautiful cove with lovely white sand. By the time the colts—or rather Cuaifeach—decided time was ripe for an approach, the mother was busy cooking sausages in a frying-pan over a camping-stove complete with gas canister. On the sand was a large table-cloth spread out with plates, glasses, cutlery, bread and butter, and in the middle, as a centre-piece, a delicious-looking apple pie, which the daughter had made. It had taken her all morning—baking in a caravan not being the easiest of domestic chores—but it was meant as a special treat for her boy-friend, who was almost as crazy about apple pie as he was about her.

The father had set up a reclining camping easy-chair and a small folding table, and was drinking beer and eating crisps whilst reading a lurid novel of the kind he saved up especially for his holiday. The son had gone out on a rock to try out his new spinning-rod—he was just attaching some of the live bait that had taken him a great effort to find in Roundstone.

The daughter had stripped off and changed into a flattering yellow bikini and was stretched out on a striped lilo, which her boy-friend was pushing around the bay. He was wearing a mask and flippers—he had planned to invest-igate the underwater life, but found himself riveted to the lilo, staring into his girl-friend's eyes, occasionally letting his gaze wander down her pretty tanned body that looked so well in the yellow bikini.

Everyone was, in other words, very much absorbed in what they had on hand, and so no one realised that two wild animals were on their way to join them. As it happened, it was the daughter who saw them first. Her boy-friend had eventually let go of both her gaze and her body and gone for a dive, and she was lazily letting her eyes wander towards land, the white sands, the green fields, the huge grey mount-ains rising on the mainland behind them. She smiled into the sun, noticed she felt slightly hungry and looked in the direction of her mother, stationed as usual, by the stove.

And there they were. Two fierce-looking beasts, standing no more than ten feet behind her mother's back, watching her acutely, as if preparing for an attack.

She screamed. The whole smiling summer idyll was shattered in an instant. The boy-friend popped up like a shot. He got it into his head that she had been stung by a jelly-fish—he had just been studying one with great interest—and so resolutely started to tow the lilo towards the shore.

"No! No!" the girl-friend sobbed. "Further out! Further out!"

He looked to the shore, saw for himself and did as she suggested.

The colts, alarmed by the uncontrolled shrieking, were galloping around the beach. By now the rest of the family had, of course, been alerted to their presence: the mother had taken herself off to behind the old ruined school-house, where she was darting to and fro aimlessly, holding the frying-pan in front of her, sausages still sizzling. The brother had climbed the highest and steepest rock he could find and was clinging to it for dear life. The father, annoyed more than anything at having been interrupted right in the middle of the most exciting chapter, grabbed his daughter's discarded red dress and, in a valiant imitation of a Spanish matador seen the year before when they were on holiday in Torremolinos, flashed it in the face of the ponies, as they came thundering towards him.

If he had thought this would scare them off, he was mistaken. It was the sort of game

Cuaifeach fully approved of. He stopped short, turned on his haunches and came charging back for more. The father made a renewed lunge with the dress, jumping clear at the last moment. This time it got stuck over the pony's head. The daughter screamed once more at the sight of her dress being carried off by a blindly galloping pony. It did fall off his head after a while—but not until he had clattered right through the picnic.

After that the colts apparently felt that they had had enough diversion for one morning, for they trotted off along the main street of the old village, towards the opposite side of the island, and didn't come back. The family members shakily reassembled.

"The sausages are cold," the mother announced with an air of grievance.

"I've lost my place," the father complained, rummaging through the pages of his book.

"My bait-box fell into the sea," the son whined.

The boy-friend's teeth were chattering, and he was covered in goose-pimples after spending so long in the cold water of the Atlantic, but he for one was not displeased. What young man wouldn't welcome an opportunity to act as rescuer and comforter to the girl he loves? But

the smug expression on his face rapidly vanish-
ed when she went over to examine the items on
the picnic table-cloth.

Big tears were running down her cheeks as
she turned round and held out the plate with
the apple pie, the pie she had taken such trouble
to make, especially for him.

She said nothing, just held it out towards
him, all the while crying silently.

It was almost enough to make him cry, too.

In the middle of the pie, going right through
it, was a large, ugly hoofprint.

* * *

When Johnny Mullen returned to collect the
family at six-thirty as agreed, he found them
huddled together at the very end of the pier,
with all their kit neat and ready to stow. They
looked cold and disgruntled, as if they had been
sitting there for a long time, waiting.

No sooner had he moored the boat than they
started to tell him, all together in shrill, agitat-
ed voices, about the ordeal that they had en-
dured on the island.

"And we are supposed to be on holiday!" the
father concluded, as if this circumstance somehow made the matter much worse.

Johnny Mullen found it hard to keep a straight face. The family stared at him incredulously.

"What's so funny?" the father demanded peremptorily.

"Sorry now," Johnny grinned, unable to control himself. "But it's Cuaifeach...he's the same as ever, it seems."

And then he laughed again.

The family said no more.

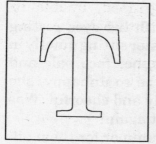he second summer the colts spent on the island was wet and windy to begin with. But then, towards the end of August, just as everyone had given up hope and the children were preparing to go back to school, the country was struck by a heatwave. It was one of those rare east winds, originating on the Russian steppes, against which even the Atlantic weather systems have little resistance to offer.

In the morning of the very last day of the summer holidays, a boy and a girl put out to sea in a curragh from the little harbour on the south side of Inishnee. They were a brother and sister, Tom and Doreen Joyce, fifteen and twelve years old. Tom was going fishing—he had heard there were mackerel in the bay. Doreen was coming with him only as far as the island where their grandmother used to live. She had brought two large baskets, for according to their Granny, there wasn't a place in Ireland where blackberries grew as plump and juicy as on her own home island.

Tom rowed steadily, with his eyes resting thoughtfully on his little sister sitting quietly in the bow with her baskets, her face pale and pinched. She used not to be so unhappy, she used to be chatty and lively and cheerful. Was he ever to see her like that again?

It had been a difficult summer for them all. Their father, after two years of unemployment, had been offered a good job as a carpenter in England. The parents had agreed that their mother with her two remaining children would be able to manage the house and the small farm for a year or two. But only a few weeks after their father departed, their mother had got sick. She had had to be taken to hospital in Galway, where she had an emergency operation. Throughout all this she had insisted that their father should not be notified. She did not want him to come all the way back again just on her account; they needed the money he was making in England and besides, she would soon be all right again. But her convalescence proved slow and painful, and it had fallen upon her two youngest children to look after things at home. She had never meant it that way, but...some things were beyond control.

"What do you want for your birthday, Doreen?" Tom asked in an attempt to cheer her up.

"I don't know..." she replied vaguely.

What was the use of saying that all she ever wanted was her father back home, her mother well again, everything back as it used to?

"Dad said to ask you. He wants to give you something real special this year."

"I'll think about it," said Doreen, and then lapsed into another of those long silences that were so unlike her.

The ponies never noticed the curragh arriving. For one thing, the thrill of visitors had begun to wear off by now, so they were less vigilant, and secondly, the curragh glided silently into a bay on the west side, stopping only long enough to let Doreen step onto the foreshore. The tide was far out, and by the time she had picked her way up onto dry land, Tom was already far out at sea putting out his line.

The girl found one of the grassy old tracks and strolled along, thinking of the stories her grandmother had told her about life on the island in the old days. She tried to picture what it must have been like when all the ruins were proper farms, when the fields were full of stock, the beds of potatoes, and the streets milling with people. She came to a crossroads with a rusty old water pump. This must be the place where they used to meet with buckets to exchange whatever gossip could be gleaned within twenty-four hours on an island this size. News from outside had also been dispensed at the pump along with the drinking water. It was here that Granny had first learnt about things like the First World War and the Easter Rising.

Doreen suddenly remembered the blackberries. She was supposed to look out for brambles. It happened to her often these days, that she set out to look for one thing and then found that she had been lost in a dream...It was a habit she must learnt to control, or she would get into trouble at school.

But before long, her attention was again diverted by something in front of her on the track. A heap of fresh dung. Were there ponies on the island? Not as far as she knew. Probably somebody's donkey...What a pity. Doreen loved ponies more than anything.

Her greatest pleasure was to go and see her great-uncle Christy in Ballyconneely. He had always kept Connemaras and over the years had bred some very successful ones. He still kept an old mare running with the herd on the vast sand dunes out at Dunloughan. Sometimes he took her there to see the ponies. He would point out the wildest ones and challenge her to get near them.

What she used to do was very calmly and quietly to go in amongst the herd and simply stay there till all the ponies came up to sniff her. Sooner or later curiosity got the better of each one of them. Once they had satisfied themselves that she did not constitute a threat to them or their freedom, the battle was won. By the time Uncle Christy returned, usually with a friend, from the pub where he had spent the interim period, he found Doreen fondling mares that no one had been able to approach for years.

"See for yersen," he said proudly to his friends. "They come quiet under her hands."

He pronounced the word "quiet" as "quite," as people do in the West of Ireland.

"Of the whole family," he continued, "Doreen is the only one got my way with the ponies."

In a flash Doreen knew exactly what she wanted for her birthday. She wanted to join the pony club in Clifden. A girl at school had told her all about it, how they were taught to ride properly, with a saddle and bridle, not just bareback with a rope halter like most Connemara kids. And they learnt how to look after a pony, not just let it off wild on the mountain. That was one thing she wanted. Then, one day, when she was old enough to work and make money of her own, she would be able to keep a riding pony of her own...

Her heart leapt at the idea.

But the blackberries! Once more she had forgotten all about them. Now she had to make a real effort. But strangely enough, she couldn't find any. Granny had said the hedges along the streets were full of them. Brambles there were all right, but not a berry in sight. They had more in the garden at home in Inishnee.

She went over to some ruined houses covered in a tangle of undergrowth and found that one half-collapsed wall was covered in huge brambles, full of large, ripe berries. At last! She started to fill one basket, allowing herself to sample only a few. Most of them would go into jam for the winter.

Then she heard a funny sort of noise, rather like someone munching away contentedly at the other side of the wall. She stretched up on her toes to see, and there he was: another creature, engaged in exactly the same activity as herself. Except that he sampled them all, there was no question of putting some aside for a rainy day. He chewed his way through the brambles, leaves and all. His lips and tongue were stained purple. Juice was trickling down the side of his mouth.

No wonder there were no berries left on the island! They had all been gobbled up by this beautiful bay pony, who was obviously very partial to them.

He looked up at Doreen, showing no sign of astonishment. Then he came round to her side, where, without further ceremony, he stuck his head into her basket and guzzled those berries, too, helplessly watched by the girl.

"Oooh!" she cried. "You pig!"

The pony gave her a surprised look from below, as if he had taken for granted that the berries were intended for him. Then he abandoned the basket, which by now was empty, and came up to put his head contritely against her chest.

Doreen soon forgave him, both for eating her berries and for slobbering purple juice all over her clean T-shirt. She stroked him and scratched him in all the places she knew ponies liked to be stroked and scratched. The pony repaid the compliment by nibbling at her hair and nuzz-

ling her affectionately. When he sniffed at her
nostrils, she sniffed back, as ponies do to each
other when they want to appear friendly.

The girl could have stayed there with the
pony all day—at least until her brother came
back for her—and she probably would have, if it
hadn't been for the sweltering heat. The mid-
day sun was baking, and the sea breeze did not
reach in here amongst the ruins. She felt hot
and sticky, and the purple stains on her T-shirt
were attracting flies. She decided to go down to
the sea and rinse it out, or she might never get
it clean again.

So she gave the pony a last fond pat, vowing
to come back and see him again later. Then she
took her baskets and made for the nearest
beach. The pony followed in her footsteps, as
closely as if she had been leading him by a rope.
She tried stopping—he did the same. She
walked on—so did he, at exactly the same pace.
Only when they reached the shore, did he trot
past her, into the water. He turned towards her
and looked at her eagerly, rather like a playful
dog waiting to have a ball thrown. Doreen felt
he was trying to say: This is fun! Come and join
me!

So she did.

As soon as she approached, he started to

splash with his front hooves in the water, soaking her all over—but that didn't matter, the T-shirt needed rinsing anyhow. She splashed back at him, and he retreated—but a minute later he was back, giving her another good sprinkling. She shooed him off, laughing delightedly. It occurred to her that it was a long time since she had heard herself laughing like that.

After they had chased each other back and forth for a while, Doreen had an idea. If she got the pony to come out with her just a little bit further, say, where the water reached her waist-high, she might try and get on his back. If he threw her off, she would merely fall softly into the sea, and if he did anything worse, like galloping off, she would simply glide off him. If, on the other hand, he had no objections...

No true horse-lover could have resisted that challenge. Doreen grabbed the long tangled mane and hauled herself up onto his back. It was warm and wet and very slippery, but she held on to the mane, and the pony stood remarkably still until he felt she was balanced. Then he turned his nose away from the shore, and before Doreen knew what had happened, he was swimming.

At first she thought they were both going to

sink like a load of granite, so strong was the pull of gravity at his massive bulk. But then, at the last moment as it were, a spasm flicked through his long powerful back, and they were not only afloat again, but high up above the surface of the water. Up and down they went, up and down, in a huge rocking movement, the like of which Doreen had only experienced once, sitting on a wooden horse in an old-fashioned merry-go-round at the funfair in Salthill. This pony was going round in circles, too—it felt unlikely and unreal, as if she had jumped on the back of a seagull and found it flew away with her.

When, in the end, the pony returned to the shore, the girl was so well installed on his back, neither of them even questioned whether or not she should stay there. She did come close to falling off once—when he stopped to shake the excess water from his coat—but after that his back was less slippery, and he stayed at a walk, though it was quite a fast one.

She had no control over him, of course—where he went she had to follow, holding on only to his mane. He took her across the island, to a field where a flock of sheep were grazing. Amongst them was another pony, a grey one, slightly larger than her mount. He came up to them and stared incredulously at the pair of them. Then, as if the sight was more than he could take, he yawned and went back to his grazing.

When Tom landed on the island, he first couldn't see his sister anywhere. She had promised to keep a look-out for him and be waiting by the shore. Slightly worried, he started to look for her, hoping she was all right. Having had to take his father's place, as it were, he felt responsible for all of them and frequently imagined things going wrong.

Then he discovered her sitting astride a pony trotting along one of the old streets. She was barefoot and bareback and had a broad smile on her face.

"Stop!" Tom yelled, aghast. "Have you gone mad altogether? Get off at once!"

Doreen made no move to dismount but the pony did stop obediently, right in front of him.

"He's real quiet," she said, patting the pony's neck.

"Quiet!" Tom snapped. "That one! It's Cuaifeach, don't you know?"

Doreen froze and, without another word, slid off the pony.

"Cuaifeach," she whispered, as if she was afraid of speaking the name aloud. "It can't be…"

"It is, I'm telling you. And you are a right eejit even to go near him. He could have killed you dead, you know. Or you could have had a bad fall, here on the stones. How could I have told Mam? Hasn't she enough to cope with already?"

The girl hung her head. For a few hours she had forgotten the worries at home. Now they came back to her. And she knew Tom was right. They must not take any risks to their own life and limb, while their father and mother depended on them.

Tom looked at his little sister. She had that silent, pinched look on her again. And only a minute ago, when she had come towards him on horseback, she had looked happy and carefree, like she used to...

"I'm sorry," he said. "But you know how it is."

"Yes," she replied quietly. "I know."

She turned to Cuaifeach, who was still standing next to her. Somehow he, too, managed to hang his head and look dejected. She put her arms around him.

"You're not as bad as they say," she whispered. "I know you're not. And I shall never forget today. Not for as long as I live."

Tom kept an anxious eye on the colt as he followed them all the way down to the place where he had left the curragh. Even as he put out, the pony made as if to swim after the boat. Tom had to raise an oar and shout, before he finally turned and went back to the shore.

Doreen saw him disappear beyond the ridge of the island.

And she repeated to herself:

"Not for as long as I live."

In the Right?

ith Cuaifeach safely tucked away on the island, Marty Mac-Donagh had looked forward to some well-earned peace of mind. But any such hopes turned out to be ill-founded, as, even in his absence, the colt continued to haunt him, over-shadowing his days like a distant, thundery cloud.

Once over the initial shock, Marty had decided to ignore that first letter from Mr Greene's solicitor. It wasn't, after all, the first time he had been confronted with a cunning horse dealer, and convinced as he was that he had been perfectly justified acting the way he did, he concluded that the whole thing was a piece of masterful trickery on the other man's part. He won't fool me, Marty said to himself, quickly throwing the letter on the fire, before Bridie saw it again and demanded to see what it contained. Later, when she asked him, he told her "it was one of them circulars."

He had almost succeeded in putting the matter out of his mind, when letter number two was delivered. Its undertone was slightly more unpleasant, with an unspoken threat between the lines. Perhaps it was the chilling formal language, Marty thought, aimed to have an intimidating effect. That letter, too, was burnt and nearly forgotten by the time the third one arrived. That mentioned legal costs and other disadvantages of letting the matter go to court and urged Marty to opt for an "amicable settlement."

He was determined not to take any notice of Mr Greene and his solicitor, Mr Cullinane, but still found himself listening anxiously for the postman's car every morning. He just happened to be hovering up on the road at the time it was due, so that he could intercept the postman before he drove up to the house. During that autumn he received four letters altogether, the three from the solicitor and one from the girls, containing a card for his birthday.

Christmas came and went, and the New Year, and Marty honestly believed that by not responding he had called the bluff of Mr Cullinane and his client. But in February a writ was delivered, a missive far more formal and menacing than anything the solicitor had come up with: "You are hereby commanded...within ten days...to enter an appearance with the registrar..."

Though Marty couldn't make heads or tails of the full contents of the writ, he did realise that it could not be dismissed as a trick. What was he to do? Who could he ask for advice? It wasn't exactly a matter you wanted discussed openly by the country. In the end he turned to the priest, Father Moran, who could be relied upon in times of distress—he really was like a good father for them all. And he listened to Marty with his usual sympathy, took in the whole story. But he had to tell him that he was in serious trouble and that he ought to have engaged a solicitor long ago.

"Solicitor?" Marty repeated bitterly. "Where would the likes of me find a solicitor? Or the money to pay him?"

It transpired that the priest had a young nephew, who had recently joined a solicitors' firm in Galway. He was shrewd, said the Father, even as a toddler he had been as sharp as a needle, and if his uncle had a word with him, he might go easy on the fees or at least accept payment in instalments. Free legal aid, unfortunately, was available only for criminal cases.

Marty went home somewhat relieved, having left five pounds with Father Moran for a special Mass.

* * *

The appointed day came, gloomy and grey, with a mean March north-westerly sweeping along the main street in Clifden. Shivering in his thin suit, Marty met up with young Kevin Moran outside the courthouse as agreed at a quarter to eleven. The courthouse was a solid edifice in grey cut stone, built in the Georgian style under English rule, designed to inspire awe and respect although nowadays it crouched in the shadow of the more recent Catholic church and had a modern fire station pressing in on its doorstep.

The courthouse had quite the intended effect on Marty.

"To think it would come to this," he sighed, shaking his head morosely. "None in our family ever got the wrong side of the law before."

"You shouldn't look upon it that way," said

young Kevin kindly. "This is not a criminal case. It's just that you and this Mr Greene have a bit of a disagreement, and so a judge has been called in to settle it for you. You're not going in there for a conviction, but for a fair arbitration. The judge is acting on behalf of both of you."

Marty gave him a doubtful look, as if concerned at the naivety displayed by his legal representative. He himself had no such illusions.

The interior of the Clifden courthouse was surprisingly shabby and run down. The plaster was peeling off the walls, the damp could be seen creeping along the ceiling. Mr Greene and his solicitor Mr Cullinane were crouching in a corner, wrapped in thick overcoats against the cold, their noses shining like purple buttons. They weren't talking, just sending disconsolate glances along the stained walls, as if they wondered how they had come to be there at all and how long they would have to stay.

Several gardai were hovering at the back of the room with their superintendent, resplendent in his uniform. Marty looked at Kevin in alarm but was reassured they were only there for the criminal cases. Then a man in a dark suit came in and sat at a raised bench up front—he was pointed out as the clerk of the court.

Other solicitors settled in their special
bench, but Kevin stayed with Marty at the back.
Then the judge entered through a door high up
at the top of the room to seat himself at a level
some ten feet above the floor. Marty had a
sudden vision of God himself peering down from
a cloud as in old-fashioned religious pictures—
except that the judge was a portly man with
silvery hair, wearing a black cloak over a well-
cut grey suit.

"He looks decent enough, don't you think?"
Kevin whispered with a wink.

Marty gave him another of those glances,
half pity, half exasperation. Was his solicitor
really so innocent, so inexperienced, that he
failed to see what was as plain as a pikestaff to
a simple man like himself? That the judge, the
superintendent, the clerk, were all out of the
same fold as Mr Greene and Mr Cullinane? You
only had to look at them, their smooth grey hair,
clean-shaven chins, the immaculate dress—
why, without the cloak you could even have
mistaken the judge himself for Mr Greene! He
and Kevin were the odd ones out—what good
was his own suit, when his hair stood up like
bristles and his face was lined and marked by
half a century of Connemara weather? Kevin,
on his part, looked exactly what he was: a clever

farmer's son who had done well in his studies, by all means, but…his suit looked as if it had been made for someone else, and the tall, lanky body inside it as if it couldn't wait to get into something more suitable, such as a pair of overalls. He had a couple of teeth missing, and the unruly hair reached down over the shirt-collar with the loosely knotted tie.

They knew it too, Marty reflected. You could tell from the way they nodded at each other in recognition—like members of the same brotherhood. He and Kevin only got a curt acknowledgement. "A fair abitration." What chance did they have?

Kevin left him to join the other solicitors, and the session started. First the court dealt with a number of applications for licences by hotels and restaurants, then with criminal cases, minor offences such as failure to hold a television licence, driving without insurance—there were about seven of those—drunken driving—four—and two cases of being drunk and disorderly. Marty found himself wishing that a really juicy case would come up to take his mind off what lay before him—but then, if there had been one, he would already have been told all about it. In Connemara you couldn't sneeze without everyone knowing.

By tomorrow, even this afternoon, there wouldn't be a soul who hadn't heard about his case...

What would Bridie say? She was at present hard at it trying to work out why he should have left home, all dressed up, on an ordinary Thursday morning.

The criminal cases were over. The gardai, the accused and their solicitors had left by and by. Only one civil case was on the list: Greene versus MacDonagh, as announced by the clerk.

Mr Cullinane stood up. In an intimate voice, as if addressing a friend, he informed the judge that the plaintiff—Mr Greene, his client—had lodged two claims for damages on two separate charges, both arising out of an incident that took place on September 2nd in the townland of Derrysilla, Cashel. The plaintiff had gone to see the defendant with a view to buying a pony foal from him. A price had been agreed, the purchase sum handed over and the pony led away. Then, suddenly, the defendant had re-appeared, demanding to have the foal back. When the plaintiff, justifiably, declined to have the deal rescinded, he found himself set upon by the defendant, who, after inflicting a deep cut on his hand, flung him into a ditch and then absconded with the pony.

The two charges were: number one, for a personal attack resulting in physical injury, mental suffering and damage to clothing, the claim amounting to a total of one thousand pounds; number two, for breach of contract, which carried a consequential loss on the part of the plaintiff, who had arranged to sell the foal on to a French customer at an agreed price of two thousand pounds. The original purchase price being fifty pounds, the plaintiff's claim for lost profit amounted to one thousand nine hundred and fifty pounds.

The judge's face changed from genial to grim as he listened to this tale. Then Mr Greene was called to the witness-box. He swore the oath glibly, settled comfortably in his seat and answered the questions from his solicitor in a calm, equable voice. Yes, he had bought the said pony foal from the defendant. Yes, the defendant had insisted on taking the foal back after the deal was completed and had attacked him when he resisted. Yes, the foal had been taken away forcibly. Suffering? Indeed, the whole incident had caused him considerable distress, mental as well as physical. Then there was, of course, the financial loss. One thousand nine hundred and fifty pounds, to be precise. He felt sure no one would find his claim anything but reasonable.

Then it was Kevin's turn to question the plaintiff. Marty was annoyed when he heard the politeness, not to say deference, with which he addressed Mr Greene. That even his own solicitor should be taken in by this crowd!

"Am I right in believing," the young solicitor started, "that the said attack was quite unexpected?"

"Totally!" the plaintiff agreed. "I didn't have a chance to defend myself. He pounced on me from behind and threw me in the ditch."

"From behind?" Kevin sounded genuinely indignant. "So you never even saw it coming?"

"I didn't have a chance," Mr Greene repeated emphatically.

"In that case," Kevin asked in a slightly different tone, "how do you know it was the defendant who attacked you?"

"How do I know?" Mr Greene scoffed. "Who else would it have been? There was no one else there."

"All right," the solicitor said placably. "Now, if I may ask you something else…the defendant did repay the purchase sum, didn't he, before removing the pony?"

"So what?" the plaintiff exclaimed petulantly. "I didn't want it back. I wanted to keep the pony."

"Naturally," Kevin agreed. "He was worth a lot of money to you. But just to get the picture clear...when exactly was the money returned?"

"When I lay in the ditch. Bleeding and helpless. He just threw the money at me and walked off with my pony."

"And what in your view, Mr Greene, could have provoked this attack? Indeed, what could have made the defendant change his mind in the first place?"

"I have absolutely no idea."

Kevin let it rest there for a moment, as if he wanted the plaintiff's categorical statement to sink in properly. A deep, effective silence settled over the court room. It was more than Marty could take.

"I thought you were meant to be telling the truth when you're under oath," he said out loud in the strong carrying voice he normally reserved for conversations across a bog or a mountainside.

This led to a sharp rebuke from the judge, who said that, if he interrupted proceedings once more, he would be held in contempt of court and possibly sent to prison. Kevin showed his displeasure by giving his client a stern look. Marty felt himself shrink to the size of about an inch.

"Any more questions?" the judge asked Kevin.

"I don't think so," the solicitor replied vaguely and sat down. He seemed to have lost his thread.

Mr Cullinane stood up.

"Your Honour," he announced confidently, "I have some evidence I would like the court to see."

He went up to the judge's bench carrying a hold-all, out of which he pulled the pin-striped suit Mr Greene had been wearing that day in Derrysilla, now in a sad crumpled state. Mr Cullinane held it out to show the judge large stains of black bog-water and a tear in one sleeve. The white shirt was also produced, complete with mud-flecks, and the handkerchief with some blood stains. The judge inspected each item, whereupon they were put back in the hold-all.

Next the solicitor presented the court with a number of certificates: one from a doctor in Dublin, who had treated Mr Greene for a cut on the hand, testifying that it had left a long-term, if not permanent scar; he had also treated bruising to his leg and back consistent with a hard thump and a fall. Another document was the receipt for the suit, made to measure the

year before at a cost of four hundred and
seventy pounds. Finally, there was a letter from
the French pony customer, written in French
but accompanied by an authorised translation,
thanking Mr Greene for his tip about the colt
foal out of the famous champion mare Veronica.
He confirmed that, if Mr Greene could lay
hands on the foal, he was prepared to pay up to
two thousand pounds for it.

"Is that all the evidence?" asked the judge.

"I trust the court will find it sufficient," the
solicitor smirked.

"Now," said the judge, stressing the word,
"what does the defendant have to say in answer
to these serious charges?"

Marty was shown to the chair up in front of
the judge's bench, handed the Bible and made
to swear on it. With his eyes fixed on the floor in
front of him, he mumbled the words so low he
could hardly hear them himself. For some
reason he felt just like the accused in the
previous criminal cases. So much for fairness,
he thought. Mr Greene had had his smart
solicitor give a beautiful speech before offering
him this chair as if he owned it. Oh well—what
support could you expect from a pup like Kevin?

The young solicitor was now standing up.

"Tell me, Mr MacDonagh," he began, putting

on an authoritative tone like his colleague, "do
you agree with the course of events as it was
related to the court by the plaintiff?"

Marty made no answer, just stared stonily at
the floor.

"You did sell him this foal on September
2nd?"

"I did," he replied sullenly.

"And after the sale was completed, after you
received the money and the plaintiff had
removed the pony from your premises, did you
have a change of heart?"

"Only because I saw him beating the foal,"
said Marty.

"Is that so?" Kevin sounded genuinely
surprised, though he must know the story well
enough by now. "You actually saw him beating
the foal?"

"He'd never known ill-treatment in his life!"
Marty burst out, forgetting all about shyness
and inhibitions. "No wonder he bit him! I'd have
done the same meself—wouldn't you?" he
added, addressing the judge.

The latter allowed himself a smile.

"Excuse me, but who bit whom?"

"Cuaifeach did."

"That's the name of the pony," Kevin filled in.

"He bit Mr Greene," Marty continued,

"because he beat him going into the trailer. There was no call for it like, he didn't play up or anything. And then, after he got bit, he went mad. Real mad."

"The pony?" asked the judge.

"No! Mr Greene. Lost his mind, like. I had to stop him. I thought he'd have him killed."

"So you threw him into the ditch?" Kevin ventured.

"I never threw him anywhere! I wish I had," Marty let slip without thinking. "But how could I, being in front of him all the time? I could only think of getting Cuaifeach away from him."

"So how did the plaintiff end up in the ditch?"

"I believe the foal must have given him a good butt," Marty said sincerely.

A sceptical look was detectable on the judge's face. Mr Cullinane's smirk was now more like a sneer.

"Are you seriously suggesting," said Kevin, "that the alleged assault was carried out by the foal rather than by yourself?"

"I wasn't even there when he got himself bit," Marty declared. "I saw it from up the hill. It was then I ran down. Just as well, so I could rescue Cuaifeach. Crazy he was…"

"That's enough," said the judge. "We've heard the story once."

"About the purchase sum," Kevin resumed. "I understand it amounted to fifty pounds. Can you tell me exactly when you returned the money to the plaintiff?"

"As he lay in the drain. I had the notes rolled up tight and I threw the roll down at him, so. I saw him take it, he can't say he didn't."

"In other words, you handed the money back after he was bitten in the hand and butted in the back? After the so-called assault had taken place?"

"I didn't think of it before," said Marty defensively.

"I have no more questions," Kevin said with a smile.

As he sat down, the judge gave him a long, thoughtful look, slightly amused but at the same time extremely doubtful.

"I have a witness to call," Kevin added hurriedly.

"Just a minute," said the judge. "I have a question to ask the defendant. It relates to the purchase sum...it seems to me very odd that you should have sold your foal to the plaintiff for as little as fifty pounds when it was clearly worth much more. Can you explain why you accepted such a low price?"

"I didn't want to sell him at all," said Marty.

"Oh?" The judge sounded suddenly very interested. "In that case, why did you?"

Marty gave a deep sigh.

"I was made to."

"Does that mean that you were in any way…" the judge hesitated "…under pressure to sell?"

"I was," Marty sighed. "Pressure is the word. I would never have parted with him otherwise. He's a fine little fellow."

Mr Cullinane had gone over to his client, and the two men were whispering together in great agitation. Kevin looked puzzled.

"Can you tell the court," the judge asked in a silky voice, "in what way you came under pressure from the plaintiff?"

"Oh, not from him," said Marty, causing instant astonishment on the faces surrounding him. "No, it was the wife. She said, if I didn't get rid of the little brute, she'd be going back with her sister in Ballina."

There was a twitch at the corner of the judge's mouth.

"I see. Thank you, Mr MacDonagh."

"I would like to call Doctor O'Leary," Kevin announced.

Marty gave up his place to the doctor and returned to his seat, while the doctor swore the oath. He was an elderly man, powerfully built, confident of manner.

Kevin got up again. He was becoming more buoyant, as the case proceeded.

"You are a general practitioner here in Clifden?" he began.

The doctor said he was.

"The court has been told that the injury sustained by the plaintiff left a long-term, if not permanent scar on his hand. I would like you, doctor, to examine that scar and then tell the court what, in your opinion, could have caused the injury."

The clerk made a gesture to Mr Greene, who, none too pleased, stomped up to the doctor. The latter looked closely at the crescent of red marks, and then delivered his verdict:

"The scar is consistent with an injury caused by a bite from a small pony or donkey."

"Could the injury have been directly inflicted by the defendant?" the solicitor asked.

"Not unless he is equipped with inordinately large front teeth. As far as I can see, that is not the case."

"May I see that hand?" the judge requested.

Mr Greene reached up to show it to him and then shuffled back to his place.

"In your view, doctor," Kevin continued, "would a pony—a pony foal, even—have the strength to knock over a man—even a man of somewhat, hm, solid build, such as the plaintiff?"

"Definitely, yes. It's amazing how people tend to underestimate the strength of a foal. In my practice, I often have to deal with kicks from foals. They can be just as dangerous as kicks from big horses."

"Thank you, doctor," said Kevin and sat down.

Mr Cullinane was already on his feet.

"Tell me, doctor, in your experience, how many times have you had to treat a patient for a bite from a horse?"

"From a horse? Never that I can remember—"

"Never!" the solicitor exclaimed triumphantly. "And yet you're standing here, pronouncing with such certainty—"

"We don't have many horses in Connemara," the doctor interrupted with as much politeness as he could muster. "However, if you had used the term "equine"...I frequently come across such bites, in the summer almost on a weekly basis. Tourists stop to give a donkey a titbit, and..."

He shrugged expressively.

"All right, donkeys. But who ever heard of a

pony biting a man?"

"Only young colts and stallions tend to bite," the doctor explained equably. "They are, on the other hand, quite prone to it."

"And how do you know, doctor? Do you profess to be some kind of expert on equine behaviour?"

"As a matter of fact, I do. My wife is a well-known breeder of Connemara ponies. We've kept them for over thirty years...including many colts and stallions."

A long silence followed. Mr Cullinane remained standing.

"Any more questions?" asked the judge.

"No more," he muttered and returned to his table.

"If you don't mind, Mr Cullinane," the judge called after him, "I think we shall have to hear the plaintiff once more."

Mr Greene looked distinctly unhappy, as he resumed his seat in the witness-box.

"Looking back, Mr Greene," said the judge courteously, "would you say it could conceivably have been the foal, rather than the defendant, that attacked you that day?"

"I can't see what that has to do with it," Mr Greene replied in a shrill voice. "It was his fault anyhow. He had no right to interfere with me or my pony. It was my property."

"That brings us on to the second charge," said the judge. "Which, I suppose, is more clear-cut."

Mr Greene relaxed a little.

"As I said before," the judge continued, "the purchase sum strikes me as being out of proportion with the market price of the foal. What are your own views on that matter?"

"Foreign contacts don't come for free," said Mr Greene. "And what about my expenses? Telephone calls to Europe, travel to Connemara...I have to cover my costs."

"Indeed," said the judge. "Any questions, Mr Moran?"

Kevin was up like a shot.

"What have you got to say to the defendant's claim that he deemed it necessary to rescue the pony because you were viciously beating it?"

"I've never heard such nonsense in my life!" Mr Greene burst out. "I gave the animal a little tap with my stick to encourage it to go into the trailer. That's normal practice. Anyone can tell you that."

"I'd like to mention to the court," Kevin said, turned to the judge, "that the defendant is known locally for a deep attachment to his ponies. To see one of them beaten would be for him like seeing his own child come under attack."

"My dear Mr Moran," the judge protested. "I doubt whether he would have sold his child for fifty pounds to a dealer."

Mr Greene and his solicitor exchanged a quick smile.

"Any more questions?" asked the judge.

"Oh yes," Kevin said, as if he had only just remembered. "Tell me, Mr Greene, how many times now have you been reported to the ISPCA for cruelty?"

"What do you mean?" the man snapped, his face flushed.

"According to my records, only three of the reports carried enough evidence to warrant prosecution. Of those, two led to actual convictions, while in the third case you were acquitted, again due to lack of evidence. Are my figures correct, Mr Greene?"

The plaintiff's scowl was formidable.

"Those reports..." he snarled "...they prove nothing. Anyone can report a person, it doesn't mean a thing."

"You're absolutely right," Kevin agreed. "Being reported doesn't mean a thing. It's the convictions that count. A man doesn't get convicted for nothing. Does he now, Mr Greene?"

There was no reaction.

"No more questions," said Kevin lightly.

"You may step down," the judge told the plaintiff, who was staring vacantly into space, trying, as it were, to adjust to the turn proceedings had taken. He stumbled back to his place with the same vacuous expression.

And now it was time for the judgement. First the judge dealt with charge number one—the attack:

"I must say," he started, "that of all unlikely defences I have ever had to deal with, this one must be one of the most unlikely. Even so, I was convinced by the doctor's evidence, and even the plaintiff himself does not rule out the possibility that the foal was the real culprit. There is still the question of liability, but since it has been established beyond doubt that the foal was in the plaintiff's possession at the time of the attack, I can't see that there is a case for the defendant to answer."

Marty wasn't quite sure how to interpret this, but Kevin's delighted expression spoke clearly enough.

"However," the judge resumed, "the second charge, for breach of contract, will have to stand. Whatever his motivations, the defendant had no legal right to take the foal back, once the transaction was completed. I therefore have to find against the defendant."

This time, Marty reflected, the delighted expression was on the face of the opposition.

"Mr Moran," asked the judge, "what exactly are the defendant's financial circumstances?"

"What you would call very poor, Justice. His income last year amounted to eighteen hundred pounds. He has his own farm—thirty acres of bogland, a small cottage with few modern conveniences. Some livestock: about twenty sheep, eight cattle. Estimated value of the farm, including residence and stock, thirty thousand pounds—but then, that's his only source of income."

"Any other assets?"

"Only the ponies—the aforementioned foal and one pony mare."

"Estimated value?"

"The plaintiff himself offered him three thousand pounds for the mare last year. Apparently he was very keen to have her. But she was never for sale—to the defendant, she is more like a member of the family."

"Three thousand?" said the judge. "That comes very close to the figure for the plaintiff's original claim. How interesting."

Then he took a deep breath and spoke rapidly:

"The plaintiff is awarded damages for breach of contract amounting to fifty per cent..."

Mr Greene knit his brow, as if he was making a quick estimate in his head, when the judge continued:

"Fifty per cent of the original purchase price, which must be deemed a reasonable profit margin."

Mr Greene's brow dropped.

"Twenty-five pounds," said the judge, "to be paid within three months, fifteen days' default. No order to costs. Court dismissed."

There was a shuffling of feet, when Mr Greene and his solicitor marched off the premises, followed by the judge and other attendants. Marty went up to Kevin.

"Can you explain all this to me?" he asked.

Kevin smiled.

"Why bother explaining? Isn't the main thing that you can go home to Veronica and tell her she's yours to keep?"

Doreen's Dream

ll over Ireland baro-
meters had risen high,
giving promises of fine,
settled weather. However, in coastal regions
the total lack of wind allowed sea mists to
linger, and on the morning of the great pony
fair, the low-lying crossroads called Maam
Cross were swathed in a milky fog.

As pony owners arrived in the early morning
to take up their positions along the road, they
and their animals were immediately swallowed
up by the thick, grey blanket: you had to almost
come upon them, before they re-emerged as
ghost-like shapes out of the mist. But other
signs revealed their many-headed presence:
the smell of fresh manure steaming into the raw
morning air, the insistent whinnying of newly
weaned foals, the shifting of restless hooves.

And, like a murmur soaring above the haze, the
sound of men's voices, as they greeted each
other, exchanged news, and negotiated.

By ten o'clock there must have been several
hundred people gathered in this otherwise
desolate spot. The crossroads were surrounded
by wide open spaces, used only for turf-cutting,
and there was only one building, or several
houses built together, serving as pub, restaur-
ant and filling station. The Maam Cross fair
always attracted huge crowds—buying, selling,
speculating or merely enjoying the occasion. To
Connemara farmers it was the main—to many
of them the only—outlet for selling their ponies.
They came here every year in October, after
harvest and weaning, as their fathers, and
grandfathers, had done before them.

The four roads leading up to the crossroads
were lined by market stalls offering everything
from scrap metal to rough walking-boots. The
main thoroughfare soon became blocked by
cars, vans and trailers and occasionally—in
fact, quite frequently—by a runaway pony,
which a dozen or so men were having a go trying
to catch. A foreign motorist stuck in the middle
of the crowd, obviously pushed for time, probably on his way to catch a ferry, sounded his
horn furiously. No one paid any attention. On

fair day trading took precedence.

A few of the sellers had come a long way from outside of Connemara: men in overcoats with well-groomed, properly tacked-up riding ponies on offer. Or dirty unkempt men who turned up with whole herds of rugged mountain ponies stunted from lack of nutrition, lousy and worm-infested. These traders were very much frowned upon by the others, and they kept a respectful distance, as if they were used to being chased away.

Otherwise the sellers were mainly local men, easily recognisable by their thick jerseys and cloth caps, and the reasonable quality of their animals. They had taken their ponies to the fair because they could not afford to keep them through the winter: grass was always at a premium and hay dear to buy. Besides, compared to cattle and sheep, ponies were not the most profitable way of using the meagre grazing that was available.

The dealers, on their part, were a varied lot: first there were the locals, identical to the sellers and frequently coming together in one and the same person. These were on the look-out for decent youngstock at a reasonable price, something they could take on—"do well over the winter" as the term went—and then show, breed from or perhaps sell on at a profit to some discerning customer. As guidance they relied entirely on their own good eye, passed on to them through generations. They usually knew all the ponies on offer, as well as their parents and grandparents, in the same way as they knew the sellers, and their parents and grandparents. One thing was certain in these transactions: there was little risk of being cheated, no possibility of information being withheld.

It was in fact at Maam Cross that Marty had picked up Veronica as a weanling. He had paid sixty pounds for her.

A typical pony deal in Connemara centres on the question of price. Negotiations follow a carefully prescribed ritual: first a discreet approach, a casual glance that must not betray too much interest. A question off the cuff: Selling, are you? Not as unmotivated as it may seem at a fair, for as likely as not, the answer will be non-committal: Ah now, I might be...if the price was right. After a good while, with a lot of discussion and inspection, the two parties will arrive at actually naming, not one, but two prices: that asked and that offered, normally with a sizeable gap inbetween. This is the time when a third man is called in to mediate: someone supposedly impartial, known and trusted by them both. He will usually suggest to *scoiltigi*, that is, split the difference down the middle, and then goes on to convince the two parties that this will guarantee both of them a fair deal. Mostly he succeeds, but it is a matter of time, depending on the stubbornness of buyer and seller. When, eventually, the price is agreed, palms are slapped to confirm the deal, the money is handed over and the pony taken away. However, it is very important that a small part of the purchase sum is given back to the buyer—"for luck." Buying without luck is asking for trouble.

Some of the local visitors to the fair were dealing just for the thrill of it, going through a number of ponies while the fair was in progress and then returning home without a pony but with a nice profit in their pocket. Seamus Lee was one of these compulsive dealers. He went up to Paddy Pat and asked him how much he wanted for his filly foal.

"Don't be bothering me, Seamus," said Paddy Pat. "I know you're not buying. And I'm not here to sell, anyway. I've only come for the competition."

Each year there was a competition for the best foal at Maam Cross.

"So you mean to say," Seamus went on, "that

you would not part with her for any money in the world?"

"It would have to be a lot of money," said Paddy Pat. "Not the sort you'd come up with."

"How good would an offer have to be?" Seamus persisted.

"At least five hundred," Paddy Pat sneered.

"Done!" Seamus cried, slapping the palm of the astonished other man. And then he pulled out a thick wad of notes and stuffed it into his hand. Paddy Pat stared at the money as if he couldn't believe his eyes. But he couldn't go back on the deal—that would have been against Connemara convention.

Before he knew where he was, Seamus had disappeared into the mist with his foal.

Only later did it emerge what had really happened: Seamus had chatted up a foreign customer in the pub and offered to "help" him buy if there was anything that took his fancy. As it happened, the foreigner's choice fell on Paddy Pat's foal, possibly on recommendation from Seamus, who then bought it on his behalf. Seven hundred the foreigner had had to fork out. That explained why, only minutes later, Seamus bought himself a nice two-year-old for two hundred, which he subsequently sold for twice as much.

Deals like that brought no ill-feeling. Even Paddy Pat, once he was over the initial resentment, had to laugh with the others and admit that Seamus had been clever. And hadn't he himself got five hundred pounds for the foal— more than he had ever expected? Of course the person introducing a customer was entitled to a bit of the profit—that, too, was part of Connemara convention.

By contrast, the middle-men coming in from outside did not meet with the same tolerance. These were often totally unconnected with the pony world, there only to profiteer from it. They preyed on the few foreign customers who found their way to Maam Cross and, however they did it, managed to gain their trust before people like Seamus Lee got to them. They warned customers of the hazards of dealing with the tricksters from Connemara, offering to "take care of negotiations" for them. This meant in practice pushing the price to the hilt and then claiming a substantial part of it back from the seller as some kind of hugely inflated agent's commission. If the seller did not play along, they simply moved on to someone who did.

A few, but very few, of the foreigners had the confidence to do their own dealing. These, on the other hand, were every pony seller's dream:

however high you fixed your initial price, intended only as a starting-point for negotiation, they tended to agree to it. The only annoying thing was it made you think you should have tried for twice as much instead. Still, it was a pity that these customers were in such short supply.

Some other welcome visitors at the fair were the well-heeled owners of Connemara studs from other parts of Ireland or even from other countries, looking for an infusion of new blood. These knew exactly what they were at, appreciated good quality and were prepared to pay for it. It was a boost to anyone's reputation to have a pony bought by one of them.

Least popular were the professional dealers, who arrived from somewhere east of the Shannon with the sole intent of buying ponies dirt cheap. They moved through the fair like steamrollers, doing their best to flatten any pride or confidence the vendors had in their products, complaining in loud voices that ponies were plain, light or crooked; back at the knee, cow-hocked, long in the back, short of rein, anything they could think of to lower the sellers' morale and thereby their prices. They rarely bought anything before the end of the day, when sales were becoming increasingly distressed: then they had their pick, choosing the best of the left-overs.

After that the saddest event of the day, really of the whole Connemara year, took place: That was when the Knacker made his entrance to scoop up the rejects that no one had wanted to buy. The Knacker had acquired his nickname, not because he actually was one, but because he was known to supply the meat factories, and no one ever chose to deal with him out of their own volition. The mountain ponies were usually the first to be herded into the big lorry parked over on the Maam road. Then followed the others, mares too old to breed, animals sick or injured, plus a large number of perfectly healthy young colts, often of decent quality, just not good enough to make the top grade of those three or four per cent that got registered and approved as breeding stallions. Out of perhaps a hundred colt foals born in Connemara, as many as eighty or ninety could go to the slaughter-house. Their breeders had no choice: they lacked the facilities to keep them over the winter—there were harsh penalties for keeping colts without due control, in case they got out and got mares into foal. And even if they could have kept them—what good was a colt that was not approved for breeding? Few people in Connemara kept ponies for any other purpose.

* * *

Late in the morning, just as the sun broke through the mist, painting the water of the lake at Maam Cross bright blue, Marty and Bridie MacDonagh arrived at the fair with Cuaifeach. They had planned to be there much sooner, but the colt had taken over two hours to load: he had been swum off the island only a couple of days before and was as yet not fully readjusted to the more civilised ways of life on the mainland.

People nodded and smiled at Marty and Bridie—the pair of them went everywhere together these days. Cuaifeach's removal from the MacDonagh household had certainly helped reinstate domestic harmony, and in addition to that, Bridie had been deeply affected when she learnt about Marty's court case only after the event. To think that her poor husband had gone around with all that worry on his mind for months, not trusting her loyalty enough to share it with her! Wasn't that what a wife was for—to support her husband in times of trouble? Had she really given him to believe that she was so unreasonable? Bridie resolved to mend her ways. Also, she was in her heart secretly flattered that Marty's ponies had been deemed important enough to be dealt with in a court of law—and hadn't the judge himself come down on their side? Everybody had been impressed by that—for over a year Marty had been immensely popular wherever he went, met with slaps on the back and offers of free beer.

Another thing—not least important—was the fact that Marty himself had somehow become more measured in his attitude to Veronica. He still looked after the mare as well as ever, still took her to shows which she usually won, but somehow he treated her more like the animal she was, not so much like an adored human being. That was much easier to live with.

The mare had had no more foals after Cuaifeach. It took too much out of her, Marty had declared. Bridie allowed herself a wry smile at that. It would have been closer to the truth to say that it took too much out of himself. She hadn't forgotten the havoc wrought by Cuaifeach's arrival. She was glad that they were, at last, getting rid of him. And this time it was for good.

Marty looked appraisingly at the colt he was holding. He had come on considerably during his two years on the island, and even though he was by no means as powerfully built as Peadar King's colt, who had come off the island with him and was also offered for sale at the fair, he looked a great deal better than anyone could have expected who had seen him as a foal. Now his appearance was that of a nice, well-balanced young pony in reasonable condition. What else could anyone wish for?

On the other hand, whether he would make it as a breeding stallion was a different matter. For that it was not enough to be faultless, he would have to be outstanding. Inspections would take place in May the following year. Marty hoped fervently that someone would come along who was prepared to take a chance on the pony till then...his breeding, after all, couldn't be better. Or perhaps someone might want him for a riding pony...he might get less contrary as he got older. There had to be someone who liked him enough to buy. If not...Marty shied away from that thought. It was too ghastly.

Sadly, Cuaifeach was not showing himself at his best. The switch back from island life had proved a difficult one. The crowds and ponies were getting on his nerves...other colts, mares, whose attractions he was just beginning to discover...Unaccustomed as he was to this kind of commotion, he couldn't help being restive.

His looks contributed to the rough impression. A large walrus moustache had grown out along with the shaggy winter coat—some sources claimed that these moustaches were a result of eating furze: the spikes tickled the hair follicles around the mouth, stimulating growth. On his face were a number of fresh cuts and abrasions acquired during a wild night in the stable, where, objecting to such confinement, he had attempted to climb out of the window. They brought to mind the face of some ruffian who had had his face cut up in a brawl.

What Marty did not realise was that the look on his own face was even more off-putting to potential buyers. He was standing there with a pained, troubled expression that bordered on desperation each time the colt played up. By way of compensation, Bridie put on a cheerful smile, so forced it fooled no one, least of all those who remembered only too clearly how she used to complain non-stop about the pony. Not that anything would have made any difference to the local buyers. None of them would have dreamt of taking on the notorious Cuaifeach. But they flocked around Marty and his colt, curious to see how he "got on."

This was even less conducive to sales. Whenever an unsuspecting stranger appeared to take a closer look at Cuaifeach, the Connemara men gleefully turned to look at him, as if keen to discover whether or not he would be taken in. Marty became more and more despondent, as the hours passed and he did not receive anything like an offer. To make matters worse, Peadar King suddenly appeared, minus his colt. Beaming proudly, a far cry from his usual dour self, he informed them all that he had sold his pony to a breeder in Waterford—who was convinced she would have him registered as a stallion in the spring. Two hundred and fifty pounds he had been paid: Peadar counted out the money in front of them, in case they doubted his word. Marty's heart sank further. It was now well into the afternoon.

But then a man—a gentleman—stopped in front of him. His clothes, a Barbour jacket, a soft tweed hat and green Hunter boots, suggested quality to Marty, though he was not familiar with labels. The man asked, in a polished English accent, about the colt's pedigree and was very impressed when he heard that this was the only son of the famous mare Veronica. How much did Marty want for him? he wanted to know.

"Two hundred and fifty pound," Marty replied nonchalantly, noting with great annoyance the titter going through the crowd behind the Englishman's back. "He'll make a grand stallion," he added.

"Well, I would probably have him gelded," said the Englishman, running his hand down Cuaifeach's front leg. "I'm looking for a nice reliable hunter for my daughter. I suppose he is as quiet as all Connemaras are said to be?"

"He has great courage," said Marty quickly, to get off the subject. He was so worried that Cuaifeach would do something untoward that he did not see the man who had come up to stand just beside the Englishman. Cuaifeach, on the other hand, did see him and must have found him vaguely familiar, because he bent down and sniffed him carefully in order to refresh his memory.

The next second he was up on his hind legs, crying as only an enraged stallion does. Then, with his front hooves back on the ground, he made a charge for the man, teeth bared, ears laid flat back against the skull.

There were screams as the crowd scattered in all directions. Marty, baffled by the unprovoked attack, struggled to get the colt back under control. But when he had managed to

calm Cuaifeach down a little, he looked around
and saw the man for himself: he was sheltering
behind a young girl—perhaps he had planned
to use her as a shield, in case the attack went
further?

Mr Greene.

"He remembers you," said Marty.

All eyes turned towards the man.

"That animal!" Mr Greene spluttered. "He's
mad! He ought to be put down! You saw it
yourselves—he tried to kill me!"

"Why don't you take him to court?" came a
voice from the crowd, followed by raucous
laughter.

"Don't think you can buy him," said Marty,
boosted by this support. "I'd give him to the
Knacker rather than to you."

"Buy him?" Mr Greene scoffed. "A lunatic
horse? You'll be lucky if even the Knacker
wants to touch him."

Only then did Marty remember his English
customer. He looked anxiously around for him.
Needless to say, he was gone, and was not
spotted again until somewhat later, when
Marty saw him lead away a strong, sensible-
looking little mare towards a waiting Range
Rover with a brand new trailer attached to it.

Mr Greene, too, soon took himself off.

"He was shook," said Connell O'Donnell, as usual telling them all something they couldn't have failed to notice for themselves.

"It served him right," said another man, who had witnessed the whole thing. "Well done, Cuaifeach!"

"Well done!" echoed the others, slapping the pony on the neck.

But Marty did not share in their banter. He was by now seriously concerned about the fate likely to befall his colt.

***

One rare visitor to the fair was Mary Joyce, a young woman who normally worked as a hotel receptionist in Chicago. She was home on holiday in Connemara, and she had come to Maam Cross with her little sister Doreen, who had the day off school, and her great-uncle Christy.

Each hour Mary spent at Maam Cross, she grew more exasperated. She had gone there with the best intentions, but somehow they were falling on stony ground. Few things can be more frustrating than seeing your good deeds not being accepted.

The night before, when she had taken her little sister aside to tell her the good news, kept until then as a surprise, she had felt rather like a fairy godmother about to wave her wand. But there had been no ovations of joy, no crack in the terrible gloom for which Mary thought she was offering an antidote. Doreen just looked at her vaguely and said, oh how nice of you. Without any enthusiasm, without even much interest.

Mary knew very well what lay behind the girl's depression. Doreen herself admitted that it was a result of missing her father and worrying about her mother's health. But the elder sister had a feeling that she brooded and worried more than was really justified—certainly more than was good for her.

To Mary herself the return home after four long, hard-working years in America had been something of a shock. Naively she had imagined that everything at home would be exactly the same as when she last saw it: the little ones, Tom and Doreen, sweet, happy, innocent kids, her mother a pillar of strength, her father comfortably settled in his favourite spot over by the window. And even though she had told herself that things would have to be a little different, she had in no way been prepared for the major changes she encountered. It upset her greatly to see her family—the little that remained of her family after the elder children left home—in such a state of despair and disintegration.

The one who seemed to have taken the brunt of it was Doreen. That was understandable, she was the youngest, the most vulnerable. What Mary found more surprising was that her mother paid such scant attention to the state her youngest daughter was in. Perhaps she ignored it deliberately, feeling that she didn't have the strength to cope with any extra worries. Or perhaps, Mary thought, with a hint of bitterness, a mother who had raised seven children couldn't be expected to concern herself with the personal problems of each of them.

One day, while the younger children were at school, she had tried to talk to her mother about Doreen.

"I wish there was something we could do for her."

"For Doreen?" said her mother. "Why?"

"Something to cheer her up. Bring her out of herself. Isn't there anything she likes doing, anything she really enjoys?"

"She used to be mad about ponies," her mother said slowly. "Dad let her join the pony club for a birthday treat. But that's over now for the year."

Mary reflected for a moment.

"Couldn't she have a pony of her own?"

"Oh Mary," was her mother's dismissive response. "Ponies are awful dear."

"When I was small every family used to have one."

"Them were working ponies. Whatever would Doreen do with one?"

"She could breed from it, if nothing else. If it were the one thing that would make her happy..."

"God love you," her mother said despondently. "I know you mean well. But at the same time, you have to be sensible."

Amazed at her mother's lack of sympathy, Mary had taken it upon herself to contact her brothers and sisters, who lived and worked far apart in five different countries. She explained to them what she wanted to do for their little sister and why, and as she had expected, they were all happy to help—except Bartley, that is, who had never had a steady job and was chronically short of cash. With her own contribution and one from their father in England, they managed to raise two hundred pounds between them. More than enough, Uncle Christy assured her, to buy the girl a decent pony at the Maam Cross fair. He would come along himself and see that they got a good deal.

In other words, all was set. The only stumbling-block was Doreen's own indifference. But that, Mary told herself, would vanish once they arrived at the fair. Of all the ponies for sale, there had to be one that appealed to Doreen enough to break the awful deadlock inside her. So much good-will couldn't possibly go wasted.

They had been among the first to arrive at Maam Cross, travelling with Uncle Christy in his rusty old banger with a trailer brought along specially for the pony they were to buy. The first few hours were devoted to looking over every single animal that was for sale, Christy being nothing if not thorough in his approach.

"We'll find you something real quiet," he told Doreen. "One you can do what you like with. It will have to be a mare of course—then you will have foals from her."

One quiet mare after another was paraded in front of them, trotted up in hand, ridden up and down the road, with or without saddle and bridle. Uncle Christy launched into negotiation over a few, but though Doreen showed a polite interest, she was unwilling to commit herself to any one pony. They left the dealing for the time being and went off to see the foal competition. A pretty dun filly got the first prize, and Christy wanted to put in a bid for her, but it turned out she had already been spoken for.

By now they were all hungry, so they repaired to the pub, where they joined a group of Christy's old cronies. The girls had sandwiches and Coke while the men downed one pint of Guinness after another, entertaining each other with stories of outrageous deals at the fair, past as well as present.

"Tried out any good ponies?" they said to Doreen, winking.

"As long as she doesn't do like Willy Walsh," said one old man.

"Ah but that was different, Willy was trying to sell."

And then followed the story about Willy Walsh, who many years ago had taken his good racing stallion to the fair. One man was very interested but unwilling to meet Willy's price— one hundred pounds, which was a lot in those days. To convince him Willy offered to give a demonstration of the horse's speed, jumped on his back and galloped hard from one end of the fair to the other. The pony went like a streak of lightning, and the customer was duly impressed. Only, the stallion, thinking some fierce beast was after him, did not stop when they got to the end but decided to run on, all the way home, to his own field near Recess.

"When Willy finally made it back to the fair," one old man chuckled, "there wasn't a soul to be seen. They'd all gone home."

"He never saw the customer again," another filled in. "Never sold the horse either."

Then they were joined by two young men, who were talking in great excitement about helicopter rides available to visitors at the fair. For only ten pounds they had had a whole new vista opened up to them: Grandad's cottage nestling in amongst the hills, streams and stone walls drawn like a network over well-known fields, wee specks of livestock adrift on the mountains, and in a yard, a minute, fiercely barking dog.

"Connemara from the air," said Mary dreamily. "That must be something else. Come along, Doreen, I'll treat you to a ride."

She felt they could both do with a break from ponies.

Christy declined the offer to join them on the basis that, having managed to keep his feet on the ground for eighty-three years, he had every intention of keeping them there for the remainder of his days.

So the girls left, and someone brought yet another round of beer.

"I hear Cuaifeach is here," one man said.

"Bringing a bit of life to the fair, he, he."

"God help us all," said another. "Is he as bad as ever?"

The other man shook his head.

"Desperate altogether. He just went for a man out there."

"I feel sorry for Marty, that's all I can say," a third man stated. "Real bad luck he had with that one."

"I wonder if the fault is with the pony," Christy mused, "or with the way he is handled. It's all a question of handling. Look at that little Doreen, now. She only has to look at a pony, and he goes perfectly quiet."

"Not Cuaifeach," said one of the men. "He wouldn't go quiet for the Lord himself."

"I'd like to try that," said Christy. "Just wait till the girls get back."

Mary and Doreen agreed that the helicopter ride was a fantastic experience. They flew through the golden sunlight of the afternoon, past the green hillsides of the Maam Valley, and the sparkling loughs over the massive grey Kylemore Abbey embedded in blazing autumn colours. Then they skirted the rugged Twelve Bens and made a sweep over the deep blue Atlantic before returning along the flat coast-land of South Connemara, as desolate as a

moon landscape. They climbed out of the helicopter, dizzy but in high spirits.

"Now all we need is a pony," Doreen said with
a laugh.

When she saw the delight written on her
sister's face as she made this remark, Doreen
told herself that she really must make an effort,
summon up all her willpower to wipe out the
picture that kept haunting her. It was a picture
lodged so deep inside her that it was difficult to
remove and replace. But at the same time it
caused her pain. It was really in her own
interest to have it banished.

By tacit agreement neither she nor Tom had
ever mentioned her reckless adventure with
the wild stallion on the deserted island. No one
knew, no one talked about it. And only rarely
did Doreen allow herself to dwell on the
memory.

But one night she had had a dream. She was
standing in front of a stone wall. Then the wall
collapsed, and on the other side was Cuaifeach.
She had clambered over the stones to join him.
He had looked at her with his soft brown eyes,
and she had put her arms around him, closed
her eyes and breathed in that lovely smell of his
sun-baked, silky coat. And she had thought,
nothing shall ever part me from you again,

Cuaifeach, nothing ever.

When she woke up after that dream, it was with a sense of hopelessness, of loss, that kept her sad and tearful for days. How she could feel so keenly the loss of something she had never had was difficult to figure out. Doreen soon gave up trying—instead she pushed the dream away, far from her conscious mind, into the deep recesses that already housed his memory.

And yet...somehow she had nursed a secret hope, so secret she had hardly been aware of it herself, that one day she would be reunited with him. She couldn't look at other ponies without being reminded of the bay colt with the wild-looking mane, the soft brown eyes...That was why none of the ponies at the fair had meant anything to her. But now time had come to return to reality, leave the world of dreams behind. Mary and the others had very kindly promised to buy her a pony. Wasn't that more than she had ever hoped for? Surely she ought to be grateful for what was on offer, select a nice quiet mare, instead of hankering after that which she could never have.

"I've been looking for ye!" Uncle Christy cried, waving his stick in the air. "I have something to show ye!"

"Another pony for sale?" Mary asked.

"Not exactly."

He led the way, followed by the girls and some of his friends, towards the green patch over at the crossroads. There, beyond the low stone wall, stood a woman and a man with a pony.

A bay colt, with a wild-looking mane and soft brown eyes.

Doreen stopped in her tracks. The woman gave her a broad smile of encouragement, but the girl did not notice.

"Cuaifeach," she whispered.

"You're not scared of him?" Christy said, his voice betraying his disappointment.

Doreen did not hear him. The colt was looking at her now, looking her right in the eye. There was no doubt about it. He knew her.

Just like her dream.

Her dream had come true.

She stepped over the stone wall and put her arms around him, scratching him gently in the place she knew to be his favourite —behind his left ear. Cuaifeach's lower lip trembled with pleasure, his eyes half-closed, and he rubbed his nose softly against her cheek.

"Didn't I tell ye?" Christy cried triumphantly to his cronies.

"Great stuff, Doreen!" someone shouted.

"Get on his back, then!" came another voice.

"Don't you be putting ideas into the child's head," said Christy. "She would, you know—if it wasn't for me being here stopping her."

Doreen turned to him.

"This is the pony I want."

Christy looked at her, uncomprehendingly.

"I want to buy him, Uncle Christy."

"Buy Cuaifeach? You're out of your mind, girl. What would you want with him?"

"I'll ride him."

"Ride him?" Christy exclaimed, as if she had suggested getting on a Bengali tiger.

The men laughed.

"I'm glad to hear you're fearless," Christy said when he had recovered a little, "but I promised your Mammy to get you something real quiet. How could I come back with a pony that is known to be the wildest in Connemara?"

"He's the only one I want," said Doreen modestly.

Christy shook his head.

"You were going to buy a mare. Have foals. You like foals, surely?"

"I don't care. All I want is Cuaifeach."

The girl's round little chin was set in a way that brought to mind Christy's brother Festy, Doreen's grandfather, long since dead. Festy had been as stubborn as a donkey. Once he had his mind made up, nothing in the world could move him. Christy knew, he had wasted much time trying to sway him.

He took Mary aside.

"What do we do?" he pleaded. "That horse is a mental. He'll kill her dead."

"It's the only one I've heard her say she wants," Mary retorted.

"Well she can't have him. A stallion! It would be downright crazy."

"Couldn't he be gelded?" Mary suggested. "Then, surely, he would calm down."

"She can't breed from a gelding!" Christy snapped. "Geldings are useless!"

"But she only wants him for riding."

"She couldn't ride a two-year-old! It will be a year, at least, before he is old enough to do any work."

"So much the better," Mary replied, unruffled. "That means we have plenty of time to have him gelded. And he will have time to settle down."

Christy looked over towards the girl. She only had eyes for the pony, who seemed to have gone to sleep with his head resting on her shoulder. A crowd had gathered around them. Christy couldn't help feeling rather proud, in spite of his misgivings.

He went up to Marty.

"All right," he said. "What's your asking price?"

"A hundred," Marty replied tentatively, assuming Christy would offer fifty and that the *scoiltigi*, with some luck, would then leave them at seventy-five.

"I offer two hundred," said Doreen.

"What?" asked Marty.

Christy turned to her angrily.

"You keep out of this."

"I'm the one buying him," Doreen persisted. "I'd like to offer two hundred."

"He's not worth it!" Christy cried in exasperation.

There was scattered laughter going through the crowd.

"He is worth every penny and more besides," said Doreen. "You did say I could choose something for up to two hundred, didn't you?" she continued, turned to her sister.

"Well, yes..." Mary replied unsurely, out of touch as she was with the art of bargaining at Irish fairs.

"Two hundred it is, then."

Doreen held out her palm for Marty to slap it.

"Never again shall I bring women and children to the fair," Christy vowed miserably.

The money changed hands, Marty gave Doreen twenty-five pounds for luck, and the colt was handed over.

"I have to warn you now," he said apologetically, "he's a bit of a divil to load."

"Never mind," said Doreen. "Would you like your head-collar back?"

In order to impress customers Cuaifeach had been decked out in Veronica's best show bridle.

"Oh yes," Marty replied. "Have you got a halter handy?"

"I don't need one."

And to everyone's amazement, the girl took the head-collar off and handed it to Marty. Then she started to walk towards the place where Christy had left his trailer. Cuaifeach followed in her footsteps like a pet lamb.

"Look at that!" cried the people in the crowd.

"You just wait till it comes to loading him," came the voice of Long John, who had appeared to give Marty and his trailer a lift back. "I know what I'm talking about. Have you plenty of rope in the car, Christy?"

"Enough to hang the brute."

They all followed after Doreen and her colt to see what would happen. A vivid discussion broke out as to how they could push, or hoist,

Cuaifeach into the trailer. It was not a horse trailer but a normal cattle cart, with a roof so low it offered nothing but discomfort to a pony, and with a floor some two feet off the ground, without a ramp. Animals had to jump, climb or be lifted in.

Doreen calmly opened the back door and asked her uncle to hold it open.

"You won't manage this on your own," he said. "We'll fix him up for you. Surely to God, there are enough of us here."

"Just let me try first," she asked.

All she did was climb into the trailer herself. Five seconds later Cuaifeach clambered in after her, lifting his legs high to get over the two-foot step. He wasn't going to let his friend go anywhere without him.

Christy quickly shut the door, forgetting that Doreen had to get out. When he was reminded and eventually let her out, she was met by a cheer from the crowd.

"I told you she has the touch," said Christy proudly. "She takes after me, so she does."

Bridie was standing in the middle of the crowd, smiling from ear to ear at the thought of the two hundred pounds.

"He's a grand pony," she kept repeating, like a cracked gramophone record. "A grand little pony. Didn't I always say so?"

In the end she believed it herself, and when Christy's banger and trailer set off in the direction of Inishnee, she had to wipe a tear from her eye.

Marty, on his part, had never felt happier.